A CHILD'S BOOK
OF
TRUE
CRIME

→⟨ A NOVEL ⟩←

CHLOE HOOPER

SCRIBNER

New York   London   Toronto   Sydney   Singapore

SCRIBNER
1230 Avenue of the Americas
New York, NY 10020

Published simultaneously in Great Britain by Random House

SCRIBNER and design are trademarks of
Macmillan Library Reference USA, Inc., used under license
by Simon & Schuster, the publisher of this work.

For information about special discounts for bulk purchases,
please contact Simon & Schuster Special Sales:
1-800-456-6798 or business@simonandschuster.com

Designed by Kyoko Watanabe
Text set in Adobe Caslon

Manufactured in the United States of America

1   3   5   7   9   10   8   6   4   2

Library of Congress Cataloging-in-Publication Data is available.

ISBN 0-7432-2512-0

For J & T

A CHILD'S BOOK
OF
TRUE
CRIME

· MURDER AT BLACK SWAN POINT ·

A whimpering echoed underground.

*A*long *the cliff the duo traveled, the wind in their fur. Kitty Koala held her breath as she snuggled against Terence Tiger's soft coat. Each giant boulder vibrated with alarm. Each tiny pebble quivered underfoot. Kangaroos bounding to the crime scene covered the eyes of their curious joeys, while overhead a flock of galahs streaked the sky a wild pink. When there was trouble at Black Swan Point, the bushland creatures were the first to know.*

A crowd of animals had gathered in the driveway of the Siddells' ramshackle cottage. No sooner had Terence arrived than the tiger pricked his sharp ears. From underground a whimpering echoed: "Boo-hoo-hoo!" Then, goodness! A little furry nose popped out of a burrow. "Why," Kitty exclaimed, "it's Wally Wombat!"

"Wally," said Terence breathlessly. "Whatever has happened?"

"Oh dear!" sobbed the usually gruff wombat. "Poor Ellie Siddell . . ."

Terence raised an eyebrow.

"Well," Wally murmured, slightly shamefaced, "I guess you've heard about her torrid personal life?"

Kitty blushed, wringing her paws. Ellie was a nurse at the local veterinary clinic, a fun-loving girl and strikingly pretty. But every local pet, recently vaccinated, had a story to tell about Ellie and the debonair vet. No matter that Graeme Harvey was married with three children—half the dogs in town returned from being fixed with some humiliating anecdote involving the couple's lunch-hour exploits.

A tear rolled down Wally Wombat's fur. "She was still a lovely girl, a lovely, gentle girl!"

Terence and Kitty glanced at each other. Rushing to the Siddells' window, they peeked inside. "Turn away, Kitty!" implored the tiger. "Please don't look!" Ellie's room, with its blue rosebud wallpaper, bore evidence of a deadly struggle. The cosmetics covering her dressing table had been strewn sideways; an evening dress hung on the wardrobe door, horribly slashed. Why, even some small china ornaments on the windowsill—a turtle, a bunny, a kitten—were cracked, or shattered to dust.

Terence Tiger covered Kitty Koala's eyes. He could hardly bear to look himself, yet somehow he managed. It was as if a wild—well, frankly—a wild animal had been at work here, the tiger thought. "Who could have done such a thing?" He stared across the horizon. At the bottom of the cliffs, black swans sang mournfully. The stately birds dipped their long necks in and out of the water, arching, straining: an ocean of question marks.

THE ROAD ALONG which Thomas and I were traveling was cut clear into a cliff face. Rude shadows of electricity poles and gum trees flashed across the windscreen. I lifted my skirt. Peeling off my panty hose, I examined new luminous veins running along the insides of my thighs. Thomas liked the way that primary-school teachers dress. Each morning, he claimed, teachers imagine what the children would like them to wear. "I have seen grown women in party frocks with ribbons in their hair." A posse of Alices who took a wrong turn. As my hand crept higher, Thomas's driving deteriorated. I concentrated on the scenery: the boulders could be tiny or like the buttressed walls of a cathedral. Some were very curvaceous, almost bulbous. "I spy a granite elephant complete with a trunk." I giggled. With my little eye, rocks also formed shapes like mouths, like tongues, like pornographic things.

Opposite these Rorschach cliffs, a huge sign, the shape of a fat court jester, appeared in the driver-side window. The jester, in medieval dress and dark sunglasses, trumpeted cheap deals on color TVs and jacuzzis two kilometers up the road. As it happened, Thomas was also wearing sunglasses and as he turned, smiling at me, a picture of the duo lined up. Thomas, so handsome in his finely cut suit, was the first person you'd expect to be doing this. He was middle-aged, for a start, with his every feature perfectly symmetrical. He looked like a lawyer, and in fact he *was* a lawyer. And from his office he'd called the staff room during recess, confirming room service for lunch. "I'm going to rent a bed by the half hour," he'd promised. "There'll be peepholes in every wall, and a scoreboard outside the door." He'd then left work early. Dumping his briefcase in the backseat, he'd driven out of Hobart—a city that still looked, from the top of Mt. Wellington, like a nineteenth-century oil painting. Sunlight soaked the clouds and purple hills soared in every direction. Hobart still looked like a triumphant oasis. And with his wife away publicizing her book, Thomas had left the city and sped toward the savages.

Laundry drying on a balcony railing now introduced the Sand and Waves Tudor Motel: a two-story slab of asbestos with exposed black beams. As a means of jazzing up the Tudor theme, each door had once been painted a different pastel color. Closing my eyes, I could almost smell the sheets. The pungency of fishermen's orgies and mermaids gone bad. "We'll rent a waterbed from some old seadog," Thomas had said. "We'll lock ourselves away, a musty Bible in the drawer in case it all goes horribly wrong." A lawyer is as interested as any criminal in how to sideswipe a rule: this affair was to be kept away from the sentimental. We only met like this, Thomas kept reminding me, to alleviate boredom. I hooked my fingers around the elastic of my underpants, and turning from him, started to slowly wriggle free. A philosopher he admired proposed that facing the finality of death helped people make something of their lives.

"Leave on your heels," Thomas suggested.

I took off one shoe and tried to slide the tiny underpants past my ankle. The trick was to act nonchalant, almost as if Thomas weren't there. He slowed, sensing I had some problem. Under scrutiny, I finished the maneuver and folded my hands in my lap.

"Bravo." Leaning over, laughing, Thomas kissed my neck. Another jester appeared, marking the driveway. Considering the motel's signage, it would be too much to wear sunglasses checking in. He kissed my neck and we drove straight past.

"Are we there yet?"

"Kate, don't pout." He leaned harder on the accelerator. "I've been thinking about this all morning. I know exactly what I'm going to do to you."

"I don't mind *that much* if we just go back there."

He paused. "We can do slightly better."

I stared at the tiny piece of black cotton now lying by my feet. I'd waited for Thomas in a back lane, eavesdropping as the little girls on the other side of the fence conducted wedding ceremonies: "Do you promise to love him for the whole of your life? Okay, then you can throw away your flowers . . . Kiss! Now, it's nine months later in the hospital. You play peekaboo." The boys were elsewhere, pretending they could fart dangerous nuclear weapons. One of my students had just been reported for pulling down his pants, trying to "bomb" an old woman walking past the school gates. The day before I'd accompanied him to the principal's office, and it made me awfully sad to see this scrawny kid, with barely anything which gave him pride, enter her room a bright-eyed hero, and leave again chastised and vengeful.

I opened my handbag, depositing my own stray underpants. "Was Veronica excited to be getting away?"

"Yes," Thomas answered. "Thank you for inquiring."
Clearing his throat he added coolly, "Of course Lucien will
miss her. Although I guess you'd know that as well as I would."

I ignored him. "How is your wife's book being received?"

"It's selling well."

Glossy copies of *Murder at Black Swan Point*, which
detailed Ellie Siddell's bizarre 1983 murder, lined the windows
of all Tasmania's bookstores. On the cover a row of swans
swam in formation; all black but for one, which was bloodred.
Then there was the title in white scrawl—after you mutilate
someone, apparently, your handwriting turns to shit. It was
supposed to look as if a psychopath, holding a piece of chalk in
his fist, suddenly decided to scrape the title along a prison wall.

I stared out the window. In the book's photos Ellie Siddell
was a slightly awkward girl, always smiling. I'd grown up in
Hobart with girls like Ellie. Girls hardwired to be sunny, even
if they were cast out—at some crucial fourteen-year-old
moment—for still being *so* immature. I imagined, later, when
all the girls were seventeen and about to finish school, Ellie
was mysteriously forgiven; and, more than that, deemed
beloved by her former torturers for being so funny and dopey,
for reacting to their teasing with a delayed, but full-blooming
blush. Ellie, oddly drowsy, with a walk so languid, just before
anyone realized a slow, sleepy walk might carry great appeal.
She finished school badly and went to stay at her parents'
country house, to look after their horses. The vet offered her
a part-time job, and her parents gave their approval. The vet
was upstanding. They knew him and his wife; she came from

an old family. And Ellie had always loved animals. She'd brought countless baby birds home, feeding them honey with an eyedropper. She'd constructed leaf hospital wards for ill caterpillars. Her parents hoped this job would be good for her confidence. Their big girl. Their big, sweet girl—Dr. Harvey would look after her. He would stand right behind her at the end of the day, taking her pretty hands in his and washing them carefully in the sink as Ellie giggled. Then he'd unbutton her blouse one button at a time, with wet fingers, before leading her into the reception area to lay her down on the couch.

"Put your shoes on, will you." The car slowed again, and we drove through a high wrought-iron gate into a circular driveway. White gravel crunched under the tires; a flurry of pebbles rose like sea spray. I caught my breath. In front of us loomed a white mansion with a wide veranda. It had been built for Tasmanian gentlefolk in the 1870s, then converted to a luxury bed-and-breakfast a century later. The building was brimming with pride: a gingerbread house, iced lovingly, bordered by candy-boughed trees. If you tried to break off a little cornice to snack on you'd be scolded.

"It's lovely."

"Yes, it is," said Thomas. "This is probably the most beautiful house in southern Tasmania." He stared into the rearview mirror, clearly agitated. "We should hurry, there isn't much time."

While he parked the car around the back, I walked toward the reception area. Topiary love hearts may as well have grown by the door. Management may as well have hired a fiddler.

Inside, the walls were painted a startling apricot. I cleared my throat. The receptionist, her blond hair in a neat bun, was also in her early twenties; she stood behind a sort of lectern.

"Do you have a double bed?" I asked efficiently. Of course, I hadn't meant to ask that. I had meant to ask for a double room.

"Let me check." She didn't smile. "How long will you be wanting to stay?"

"We're not absolutely . . . we're just, just not absolutely sure."

The Persian rug gave a slight electric shock. I glanced at the potpourri arranged in crystal dishes; the lace doily and single rose on each of the dining room's tables. Then I turned. A three-legged cat was dragging itself sideways up the black-wood staircase. The receptionist tapped her fountain pen against the register: the cat lifted its two front legs up a step, then hauled up the third leg. I could hear Thomas cautioning, "This is just a fuck." But as the chandelier sent confetti light across the high-gloss walls, I wondered if his warnings were directed not to me, but to himself. The cat made its turnoff. And the receptionist, tapping her pen, noted that almost every room was vacant. She looked offended as she licked her finger, with its shiny buffed nail, and counted Thomas's cash. "If your stay is cut short, if you don't stay the *night*," she enunciated carefully, "please leave the key on the desk."

It took me a moment adjusting to all the Victoriana. I'd been imagining a motel room: mirrors with 3 A.M. pores, a notepad by the phone full of strangers' doodles. Instead there was a spinning wheel in one corner and a four-poster bed. Whoever had decorated felt they understood wallpaper very intimately. Even the light switch was bordered with a lacy pattern, even the row of gilt picture frames. The frames, suspended with pink velvet ribbon, contained sepia photographs of children, all ringlets and rose-tinted cheeks, posing next to a penny-farthing bicycle, a rocking horse.

"Darling, it's perfect," Thomas said, grinning. He excused himself and disappeared through the door stenciled in sweeping cursive: *Lavatory*. When I was alone, I walked over to the dried flower arrangement. Above the brittle petals was a mirror, with a short young woman inside its frame. She looked like she'd broken into her mother's makeup case, trying to make her eyes more almond-shaped. Someone had shown her a curling wand and her dark hair was tousled expertly on one side, but the other—where she'd practiced—lay flat. Behind the flowers, like the consolation prize, hid a plastic kettle, coffee sachets, and a mini-packet of cookies. Opening up the cellophane wrapping, I stuffed both the cream-centered biscuits in my mouth. I could hear Thomas whistling. He whistled well.

When we first started trysting he played music that, he said, reminded him of me. He brought sweet things: chocolate mice and gingerbread men (waiting to see where I took the first bite). Once he gave me a box of perfect peaches. Then, handing over a knife, he requested that I let him watch. "Pretend you're alone," he said. And this seemed hilarious. I camped it up, eating peach straight off the knife; rubbing the fruit on my wrists like cologne. I thought this was the game itself—and that by pretending to be sexy I was canceling out any sexiness. Another theory proved wrong. After I dissected the peach he still wanted to undress me.

The toilet flushed. I crammed the cellophane behind the kettle, and Thomas reemerged, moving impatiently to draw the lace curtains. My heart was beating fast. I stood in the room, my mouth full of vanilla cookie crumbs, watching him. I needed to brush my teeth, but my thoughts were on loop; *it's too late to leave, to pretend to feel ill.* Downstairs I heard somebody laugh. Reticence had arrived to match the wallpaper. For a split second, my new modesty made me want to call my parents, and ask them to come and pick me up.

"Aren't these dried flowers pretty?"

"Yes." Wet fingers started to unbutton my shirt. "They're pretty."

I wished I really were a little girl. Little children can transform themselves from magic birds into flying strongmen. At play, children wear intense expressions and make a range of hero noises; common is the windy *vroom-vroom* of their invisible jet plane's ignition, the *neeeow* or *p-queeww* of lasers shooting from soft fingertips. Running with their arms stretched straight ahead, the children become the most powerful and beautiful—the most super—people in the universe. They believe the ordinary properties of objects irrelevant; for example, this Victorian four-poster, covered in cream lace, could have been a hospital bed. Typical social roles didn't necessarily shape the imagined world either, so Thomas could have been a doctor who was giving me a checkup; and speaking out of turn when, reaching my black-and-pink bra, he said casually, "That's a nice print."

The bed was huge, pneumatic. A reproduction mahogany

stepladder clung to its quilted flanks. Thomas held my hand and I walked up the steps. He then undressed himself, looking all the time so serious. He took off his business shirt; he unzipped his trousers. Before we made love he would always hang his trousers, and then I had to close my eyes. It was too much seeing him standing there in high, black business socks. "Just smile a little"—he thought he had to be stern with me; he'd told me that. Otherwise I didn't treat things with enough gravitas. We'd get into bed and I'd start to laugh. "Just smile a little because we are both about to be naked."

Thomas had the tanned legs and white arse of a summer person. His body was not like the boys' bodies with their easy muscles I'd seen before; but in the blue light, the lines on his face were almost smoothed away. As we kissed I tried to taste his age. His lips were unexpectedly soft. He smelled smoky although he did not smoke.

"How do I look?" I asked, teasing.

He shook his head. "Gorgeous."

"Do I look *lush*?" Lush seemed like a better thing to look.

"No," he said firmly, "you're gorgeous." He covered my eyes, his hand scented with almond soap. "What can you see?"

"Your palm. It smells of marzipan."

I was supposed to whisper to him. He liked this. He liked this even though my story lines were simple: *We're in a meadow surrounded by poppies,* I used to tell him in the beginning. *Can you feel the petals against your skin?* Or: *We're on a train and the sun is coming up, flickering through the trees.* Now the content had changed. I said things he must have wanted to hear because these things shocked me. The Puritans, all busily fornicating through a hole in a white sheet, had the right aesthetic. If you acknowledged this enterprise was dirty and wicked from the start, no one had to try to be transgressive.

Thomas kissed my neck. "Where do you think we are?"

"I don't know."

He sounded impatient. "Do you think it's *hot* . . . where we are?"

I closed my eyes. Outside, cars were driving along the highway. There was a kind of roar every time they passed the house's force field, so constant it was like listening to the sea. "Pretend I'm holding a shell to your ear," I whispered. "Do you hear the static?"

"Yes," he moaned quietly.

I rolled on top of him. "What should I do with the shell?"

"Put it down. Dance for me."

I laughed.

"Dance, I would like that."

We were high off the ground. It wasn't dark enough, and the room smelled odd. I closed my eyes. Humming a line of music, I raised my hands above my head.

"Move your hips."

I hummed the music and rocked back and forward, dancing. If I had opened my eyes I might have seen him smiling. In this room, strangely blue, I was making him happy. I always wanted to make him happy, then some part of me rebelled. "There's a fringe of seaweed knotted round my waist." I rose a little and, arching my back, suggested slowly, "I'm very close. Each bauble brushes your face as I swivel my hips." I thought further; "There's a rainbow bird on my bare shoulder."

A moment of silence. Introducing the parrot, I realized, was the first mistake.

Thomas gazed at me with an intense, hungry look. He inhaled. "Little girl, I can smell your skirt."

I brushed hair from my eyes. "And does it smell of sea air?"

"Yes."

"Does it smell *salty?*"

"Aha"—he smiled—"a dusky scent."

I ran my hands along his chest. "Pretend you've captured me and taken me to your island of black swans . . ." I leaned down and whispered, so close my lips touched his earlobe: "And the sun is beating down on us. And no one can see us lying here, only the animals and they're all fucking, too!" I giggled. "It's like a zoo of fornication!" I sat up again and raised my arms, like wings, above my head. "The black swans, their feathers are beating against the water—*beat, beat, beat*—and the girl swan is shrieking *No! No!* and the boy swan, his red eyes are so intense." I curved my arm, hiding behind it like a cape. "And when she folds her long neck under her grand wing"—I paused—"it looks like she's been beheaded . . ."

"That's not funny." He sighed and jerked slightly, forcing me to roll off him.

"It was a joke!" I clutched his arm, then lay still, annoyed. "A little joke." Light seeped in the curtains' edges. We lay next to each other in the half dark, listening to the cars passing by on the highway. Cicadas continued their slow drone, and I felt bad. Thomas looked like a young boy with skinny muscles on his arms and undeveloped pectorals. I was lying in bed with a little boy. In this game his age kept morphing: sometimes when he kissed me he looked ridiculously old. So old that he started to look young again; because he had the pleading expression, tinged with the beginnings of disappointment, that a child with ridiculous faith uses on an adult. The potpourri, all the floral wallpaper, was still Romance, wasn't it? Despite his high regard for amorality, he couldn't help being kind. Usually we trysted in the house where I was living; my family's old beach house. This was his attempt to make renting a room nicer for me.

"Are you angry?"

"No," he said, quietly.

"Thomas, seriously, can you smell something?"

"It's rising damp." He got out of bed, slowly, as if he had a sore rib. "This place was probably built on swampy land." He reached over for the complimentary bathrobe, a brown, terry-cloth model hanging from a hook on the lavatory door.

"You're the man with the furry tan," I told him as he slipped it on.

He smiled thinly and, walking into the bathroom, left me in the whirlpool of sheets. I lay completely still, listening to the water running. Had he been here with her? If I checked the guest book would Veronica have written some soppy note full of exclamation marks? *Olde worlde charm! This brought the magic back after 11 years of marriage! Thanks!* Or else something literary about rage and potpourri. Or else something completely self-serving:

Female killers are more fascinating and more repulsive—koob ym yub—*even though you'd think women would make better killers because they're so used to blood. They know what blood feels like on their skin or their skirts, women know how quickly it spreads everywhere and how to clean it out of clothes*—KOOB YM YUB—*always use cold water; get to the stain quickly.*

A series of cracks, like tiny lightning, streaked across the ceiling from the plasterwork rose. What about a little drink? Why wasn't there a heritage bar-fridge stocked with absinthe and gruel? The water was turned off abruptly. "I'd better check my messages," a still-dry Thomas announced. His clothes were hanging neatly over the armchair, whereas mine had been bombed around the room. He knew exactly where his phone was, and picked it up to dial some numbers. I loved when he did his lawyer-talk, all stern, in a very nuts-and-bolts way. I loved this, when he called into the office and spoke to everyone like they were imbeciles.

His brow furrowed. "There's a message from Veronica."

I made a face at him.

"Listen, I'm sorry, Kate, but it sounds like there's been an emergency." He went into the bathroom to speak with his wife. The door was open a few inches. "Sweetheart," he whispered loudly. "Sweetheart, what's happened?" A pause. "Hey? Is Lucien okay?"

I stretched. I arched my back and it was then I really noticed the sepia photograph above the bed. A small boy with a bowl haircut stood by a penny-farthing bicycle. The boy suddenly looked exactly as Lucien would, if he were wearing a lace collar and knickers. Lucien was Thomas and Veronica's nine-year-old son, a sweet, complicated child. It was probably true he'd been my favorite before I'd even met his father. Listening to Thomas, I realized I was still slightly upset. That morning Lucien had come to school and all the other fourth-graders had laughed at him. He'd just had a growth spurt and, wearing short shorts and a blazer over his T-shirt, he'd looked like a visiting dignitary with very white thighs. "I like being different!" he'd called out theatrically. "Wearing clothes that don't match." It was staggering how clearly his character, including eccentricities, had been etched. I worried for him. He was very sensitive, and the sensitivity was intelligent: he had an excellent radar.

"Oh no!" Thomas groaned. "Oh no! They had no right. No right! . . . But you're in the hotel now? . . . Hey, hey, stop crying."

I tried to piece the conversation together: Veronica must have also been in a hotel room somewhere. And hopefully Lucien was safe; sitting, reading science fiction, in the half hour before class.

"Why don't you try to rest?" There was a pause. "All right, sweetheart, I'll call you later." Another pause. "Me too," he murmured.

Thomas waited a moment before walking back into the room. He sat roughly on the edge of the bed. "Veronica was speaking on a panel about her book. Someone stood up during question time and abused her."

"How awful."

"Some vigilante," Thomas spat. "On about journalistic truth!"

Buoyed, I got out of bed. My clothes were in a flurry of rude postures all over the floor. Inside-out sleeves strangled each other; a skirt was hitched up, in flagrante delicto. I found my panty hose, and wriggled one straight leg in, then, rocking, the other straight leg.

Thomas watched me, sighing. "You look like Charlie Chaplin." He reignited. "I don't know what these arseholes want! The book is published with a disclaimer!" He put his head in his hands. "It is so damn controversial. Just yesterday journalists were around the peninsula muckraking, asking any old fuck for their opinion."

"And what do the old fucks say?"

"They say: *we hate this!*" He waited a beat. "Et cetera."

I knew how they felt. Thomas was sitting on the edge of the bed in the brown dressing gown, waiting for some response. I stayed silent, wondering how he'd feel if something happened to me. According to *Murder at Black Swan Point*, the morning after the girl was killed, Dr. Graeme Harvey woke slowly and realized his wife was missing. His head ached. He'd arrived home the previous night, late, and they'd fought badly. Margot had pushed him into admitting the truth; then, rageful, she'd struck at him with a bottle. "Not everything has to be so momentous," he'd told her stupidly, the blood streaming down his cheek. And she'd stood there weeping, harder, for seeing him bleed. The next morning, Dr. Harvey, unaware of what he'd slept through, probably lay in bed angry. When his wife decided what was bad, when she decided *he* was bad, she claimed every inch of moral ground, and there was now not a balding shrub to cling to, not a single slapstick face-saver. He lay still, listening for his daughters, then listening for Margot in the kitchen. The television was on. His daughters were not supposed to watch television first thing, but as the cartoon's tune rang through his bedroom, he realized they must have been sitting there, spooning sugared cereal into their mouths: impressions of the brain-dead. He heard the stupid music and lay there for one more minute, not yet ready—I bet part of him was too tired, already. In the act of getting vertical, it was settled: he was a prick.

I watched Thomas, his head in his hands, but imagined

Dr. Harvey. Loping to the bathroom, the man must have groaned. There was a trail of blood on the bedroom carpet. Blood, far more than he'd remembered, was also on the bath mat and on the tiled floor. It was on the taps; and the basin; and flecked on the mirror. "Margot!" He strode out into the playroom, and his daughters rushed to turn off the television. "Where's your mother?" The girls saw his face, all cut. They whimpered. He looked out the window: the car was gone. The girls were whimpering. He walked back to the bedroom and called the police.

Eventually Thomas glanced at his watch and sighing, stood up. Taking my skirt from my hands, he knelt before me. In his act of special prayer, he eased down my panty hose.

"We don't have time."

Thomas pressed his mouth against my thigh. I was trembling. His kisses began to escalate. My legs buckled and I lay down on the prickling rug. I could see the sturdy slats of the bed; I could see under the frill of the chair. Now we were both concentrating. But I'm like an old record—*Be my guest* is the signature song; *Please go away,* always on side B. Dumbness arrived in a series of shudders. I lay moaning and inside my head felt the spinning of a reel. The grainy black-and-whites of Ellie Siddell's body slid behind my eyes. I winced. She had been stabbed repeatedly in the face; some of her teeth were found scattered round her on the blood-soaked carpet. And the nauseating detail that's always mentioned in tones completely hushed, an inverse fanfare: her throat was cut so viciously she had been beheaded.

· MURDER AT BLACK SWAN POINT ·

Scouring every hidey-hole!

*K*ingsley Kookaburra flew high over Black Swan Point. He *saw the beach clotted with piles of leathery seaweed; he saw the yellow dunes rising to meet the cliffs. In the search for Margot Harvey, Terence Tiger had requested the bushland gang scour every hidey-hole for a bread crumb of a trace. There was Wally Wombat analyzing tire prints. Higher! There was Percy Possum questioning a witness. Higher! Higher! There were the swans, black specks on the shimmering horizon, still singing their dirges . . . Could Kingsley fly high enough to avoid Graeme Harvey's grief? It lurked like a mushroom cloud over the peninsula. Oh, it was jolly awful losing someone for whom one felt love.*

"I did this," the girl's paramour must have been thinking. "I did this to you." He probably wished he were the one who'd been killed, Kingsley imagined. He would wonder, "Were you sleeping? Were you awake? Did Margot steal up on you? Did you fight? Was it dark? Did your eyes have time to adjust?" When studying a crime, the kookaburra was not shy in peeling back the surface to uncover a protagonist's most basic emotions; psychiatric profiling provided rich ore indeed—"I should have known this would happen," Graeme Harvey would think as his children cried for their mother. He'd want to hate his wife, oh certainly, but silently that man would scream: "Why couldn't she have taken the knife to me!"

Kingsley began his graceful descent. With his keen eyes he noticed the mise-en-scène of a silverbark leaf far below. A male phosphorescent insect offered a female of his species food, then took it back after copulation so as to gain energy for another sex partner. . . . All through nature there were such stories of deceit and betrayal. Watching animals at their best and worst had taught the kookaburra a great deal. It was difficult to admit our core desires were hammered out long, long ago in the ancestral environment, and Kingsley could not easefully align himself with evolutionary psychology. Still, he'd recently read a study of working-class Germans, which found that 72 percent of the men expressed a desire for extramarital sex, compared to 27 percent of the women. Kingsley laughed slyly. "Bloody Huns!" Could one conquer one's instincts? Perhaps it was innate to men's sexual psychology to be so disposed toward seeking variety. Women's desires and fantasies simply didn't seem as intense.

But wait, down, far below, there was a snake! Kingsley was hungry. It was getting ever harder to eat well round here—his relatives had even taken to raiding suburban goldfish ponds. In a grand flutter of wings, the kookaburra swooped and grabbed the snake from behind, smacking its poisonous head again and again against a rock. He laughed his maniacal laugh. "Merry, merry king of the bush is he!" Kingsley, his belly now full, flew over the cliffs, past rock—bruised purple, bruised red—swollen with history. Through the mad blue of sky, he soared. "Oh, why can't we just love each other!" the kookaburra cried.

THOMAS RETURNED the key to the receptionist while I waited in the low silver car. Without the air-conditioner in operation, there was a sauna feel, and I sat in the hotel's staff parking area sweating out my sin. Thomas had parked next to a rust-eaten Dumpster. Soon enough a young guy with a long shock of fringe and a loping walk came out to throw away some cardboard boxes. He stared at the expensive car quizzically, and I ducked down as if I'd lost something. Opening up the glove box, I rifled through Thomas's stash of postcoital products—a comb, some cologne, a hip flask—until I found a packet of mint breath fresheners. Three for me, and when Thomas finally opened the door, I leaned forward and placed one on his tongue.

"Fucking in a hotel?" he lisped, adjusting the seat belt. "How many stars?"

"Three."

"That's not so bad." He turned the key in the ignition.

"Three out of a hundred."

The tires ground against the pebbles. We drove too fast down the manicured driveway. Trees bent back as we sped by. Lining the road, these gnarled tea trees and banksias—writhing, mournful—made me nervous. They always reminded me of thin-limbed performance artists pretending to be ghosts.

Thomas smacked the steering wheel. It was impossible to see around the next corner, the highway was one-laned, and a logging truck crawled ahead. Bark and wood chips flew toward us. "Jesus, Kate. Why didn't you turn on the air-conditioner?" We were so close we could count each log's concentric rings. "I've got to get this young lady back to school!" he complained. "For the sake of my boy's education!"

There was some truth to this statement. The Marnes had moved to Endport the previous year so Veronica could work on *Murder at Black Swan Point*. Thomas commuted, spending the week in Hobart, the weekend with his family. After the book's release, in June, his wife had wanted to return to town, but he'd convinced her it was unfair switching Lucien's school midyear. Also, as he liked pointing out to me, it would have been more difficult setting curricula at a Hobart private school.

At first Thomas and I had promised not to discuss Endport Primary, but after a while our meetings took on the charge of a highly exclusive Parent-Teacher Association. Thomas had realized this was a good way to monitor his son's progress. Instead of love letters, he sent me detailed notes proposing different lessons for the children. He felt strongly they should be told the truth about their local history. I agreed: yet at the beginning of the year I'd skirted around the issue of genocide, by only asking the kids to write their own versions of Aboriginal Dreamtime stories. The results had been cute, but hardly unflinching: *How the kangaroo got her jump. How the kookaburra got his laugh*—soon enough the children's efforts became slanted toward their own ethnic preoccupations—*How the white man was created.*

It seemed difficult bringing it home that this white man was a convict; that Tasmania was basically conceived as a jail girt by sea. Thomas was undeterred. Due to his campaigning, the children learned that the state's main penal settlement, the nearby Port Arthur, was named in 1830 after the state's lieutenant governor, Sir George Arthur. Sir George—an evangelist who believed his calling was to make men moral—had visions of a prison to end all prisons and geology conspired. The Tasman Peninsula, where the children had all grown up, where Thomas and I were now driving, was a thin strip of land, connected to the rest of the island by an isthmus, less than one hundred yards wide, named Eaglehawk Neck. Port Arthur, where convicts were ground into God-fearing citizens, was built at the south of the peninsula. Most of these men were unable to swim, and, to counter fantasies of overland escape, the neck was lined with vicious dogs; white cockleshells to highlight trespassers; and offal. The guards were said to dump offal on the surrounding beaches to encourage sharks. The same year that Port Arthur was established, over two thousand settlers and soldiers marched through the Tasmanian bush in a closely packed line, trying to force the Aborigines through the neck, where it was figured—incorrectly—they could be rounded up and captured.

Thomas suggested, in early July, that the children practice their letter-writing skills by sending postcards to the Tasmanian parliament, urging that the Aboriginal Land Acts be passed. Prime Minister Keating had just unveiled his plans for a republic, and Thomas was feeling reckless. Afterwards the children came to school crying because *their* parents had reeducated them. They were going to lose their backyard, and therefore the new swing set or trampoline. "Why do people tell each other stories?" I'd asked the class. I'd figured we could analyze the motives of storytellers such as their parents. No one had spoken. "Why do you think the Aborigines made up tales about how the kookaburra got his laugh?" The children agreed it was because things were really boring in the old days and everyone was bored. "Why do *we* use the expression a cat has nine lives?"

> Henry: *Because if it jumps off a building it has a better chance.*
>
> Danielle: *Cats always land on their legs. Dogs always land on their backs.*
>
> Darren: *But if you just come up and shoot your cat it dies.*
>
> Anaminka: *Its spirit would come out, only it might turn into a mouse.*

The exercise had perhaps been slightly abstract. I'd decided to be more straightforward: "When do you think it's appropriate to lie?" I'd asked, standing still to bear witness. Each inquiry I made was like throwing a pebble into the sea. The children's answers were rough but brilliant, vast in meanings unrelated to the pebble.

> Henry: *I don't exactly lie, but sometimes I hide my sister's stuff and she says, "Henry, have you seen my stuff?"*

Billy: *And you go, "No."*

Henry: *And I go, "Have you looked in the lounge room?"*
But it's in the bedroom.

Billy: *You could do that, but you wouldn't hide anything*
serious. You wouldn't hide your sister's dress on a
Sunday night.

Darren: *She'd have to go to school with no clothes on!*

"This is a fucking farce," Thomas muttered.

The logging truck still crawled ahead. We passed a turnoff to Black Swan Point and continued on to Endport. These two towns, only fifteen kilometers apart, were both seedlings of Port Arthur. In the late 1870s, after the penal settlement was closed down, Endport's newly righteous settlers painted the convicts' unmarked gravestones white. In the cemetery they now lay around shattered; kids—maybe even the dead's direct descendants—had nothing better to do. Once in the town pharmacy I heard the chemist bellow to a patient, "You might think depression is embarrassing, but there are *streets* full of depressed people out here!" Endport's most exciting event was a competition raising money for the local hospital. People raced hospital beds down the Main Street with somebody in each bed. It couldn't be a child under twelve in your bed; perhaps for the child's safety, or in case another contestant had a very fat person in their bed.

Thomas's briefcase was on the backseat. "Will you have to work this weekend?" I asked.

"Not too much."

"You should try to have some relaxation."

"We'll see."

I stared out the window. Every house was a front for some auxiliary service. If there was an old nag in a paddock, there was also a placard reading "Trail rides." A chicken: "Fresh eggs" or "Manure." Off-season these coastal towns flaunted the fact that no one loved them—pavements were sprayed a blotchy gull-shit gray; a few letters in every neon sign switched off; and roadkill deposited around each bend. "It's just grotesque," I announced. "If you were a tourist you wouldn't need to go to a wildlife park; our fauna is all displayed by the side of the road." It was like dipping a toe in the water to test how cold: Thomas said nothing. He was thinking of his wife's phone call. "My grandmother," I told him, "had a recipe in her cookbook for wallaby stew."

"*The Roadkill Cookbook*." He sounded unimpressed.

I laughed. "'Don't count on finding roadkill for those last-minute occasions when friends drop round. Always keep something in the freezer, so you're not left red-faced.'" Ahead of us the truck inched up the hill. The air smelled of diesel fuel and freshly cut eucalypt. "*The Roadkill Cookbook* would stress, 'Don't be foolish retrieving the kill.'" I waved my arm leisurely out the window. "'We don't want you to get hurt too.'"

"This is a farce," Thomas repeated, but I had regained his attention. He turned on the car's CD player. Sometimes when I was contrary he would choose a piece of music which he thought described my ill temper. I knew nothing about music, but at first had taken slight offense at what I perceived in his selection to be a lack of intensity: often a coltish joy was too close to the surface. Didn't bearing the moral weight of this affair call for more gravity? Some jarring notes? I waited as Thomas found the right track, and made a pledge to be better behaved. Perhaps the music's giddiness had not been indicting me. It was him saying, "You make me light." A string of notes now sounded from the car's speakers, and Thomas turned to catch my expression. I listened: it was slippery. Behind every loveliness was something harsher. I thought of a swimmer too far out; then a force that kept pulling him further. The music spoke of an undertow.

The way Veronica told the story: after Graeme Harvey sounded the alarm, the police drove immediately to the Siddells' property. All the curtains were drawn, but they found the back door unlocked, and walked into the dark house. The bedroom had been vandalized and the girl lay on the floor—a blanket covering her head and torso. The warning was immediately broadcast that Margot Harvey was homicidal and possibly suicidal. Airports were notified; boats to the mainland; all investigated. In the days after Margot's disappearance, Graeme Harvey stayed in his bed, deep in shock. He was apparently not the type of man one expected to see shattered. With his perfectly regular demeanor he'd always seemed unshakably confident, but in just one night he'd lost everything. I suppose relatives cared for the Harveys' children elsewhere, while pathologists scoured the house. Another team was tending to the murder site. It was imperative the police establish which of the protagonists had bled and where. Routine scrapings were taken of the blood in the kitchen, the site of Mrs. Harvey's bottle attack; scrapings were taken of the blood on their bedroom and bathroom floors where she had tended her husband's wound. In the living room Dr. Harvey was interviewed, but was barely able to speak. After the police were finished, he probably had to lie, dosed out, in the bed he'd once shared with his wife.

Eventually the Harveys' station wagon was found abandoned near the edge of the Suicide Cliffs—a treacherous stretch of coastline surrounding the ruins of another old penal settlement. A park ranger discovered the car thirty-six hours after Margot's disappearance. No one could be sure how long it had been there. The ranger was doing a routine check, and had noticed the car where parking was not permitted. He opened the door carefully. There was a woman's handbag on the passenger seat. He radioed the registration to the local police. A crime squad searched with dogs; volunteers combed the area. No trace of the missing woman was ever found. It was presumed Margot must have driven straight from Ellie Siddell's house to these cliffs, that she had then jumped into the backbreaking waters below.

An overtaking lane appeared and Thomas, his foot flat on the accelerator, passed the truck with an expression of great triumph. The music surged. It grew into something horrible. And then there was more roadkill. A terrible spray of red across the bitumen was somehow connected to the long, furry tail of a wallaby. I gave a girlie screech. Amidst the gore I could recognize something solid like we once dissected in high school science. "I'm sure I just saw that animal's heart, or at least one of its vital organs!" I shuddered. "Thomas, I felt so ugly in that hotel room!"

"You certainly didn't look ugly."

"Be serious!" I covered my eyes. "I can't stand this much longer."

Thomas said nothing.

I waited. "Did you hear me?"

"Yes, Kate," he said calmly, "but I don't particularly want to."

"Well, I don't want to say it, but all this sneaking around, the lying." I watched him from behind my hands. "Oh Thomas, I'm crazy about you, but you know . . . I just don't want to be dragged into something awful."

"Lovely, you already have been." He swerved into the right-hand lane. "You're right in the middle of the something, and it's not so awful. It's called *cinq à sept*, five to seven, or in your case *le dejeuner;* it's when half the unmarried women leave the office to sleep with one of their married co-workers."

"Stop speeding."

He didn't slow down, but grinned. "Kate, in the old days adultery was de rigueur. They say drunk women lay all over these roads; poor hopeless women of a fertile age sent down to screw the convicts." He paused. "It would have been sensational. Just imagine this island like a swinging cruise ship. Everyone surrounded by water, unable to leave."

"Maybe," I thought aloud, "we should tryst on a boat."

"I don't really like boats."

"Seasickness?"

"Imagine being in prison," Thomas said, "except you could also drown."

Outside small tenacious plants—pigface and beard heath—clung to the sides of the cliff. We were on the edge of town, and I went to work straightening myself. Pulling up my skirt in a businesslike manner, I tried again to put on the panty hose. Thomas glanced over at my bare thighs, and shook his head. "This would be your report card: 'Miss Byrne started the date with great promise. Within a very short time she'd impressed the class with her willingness to undress.'" He raised an eyebrow. "'Not very wise when someone's at the wheel, but we commend her spirited performance. Especially,'" he stressed, "'since despite her excellent practical skills, and vivid imagination, she has a poor attitude toward her studies.'" I struggled with the hosiery. "'Consideration of the group: poor. Her ability to play cooperatively: borderline. She does work well with her hands.'" He paused. "'She would make a good clay student.'"

I flicked down the sun shield. In the mirror I now looked wild. There was a hairbrush and lipstick in my handbag, but I felt a sudden apathy. The land outside was swampy, built up with holiday houses on stilts made of prefabricated board. By the start of January, everything would be decorated with wet beach towels. There would be people flip-flopping everywhere, laden with inflatable chairs and giant umbrellas; refugee clowns carrying everything primary-colored they'd ever owned.

Nausea lodged low in my belly. I wished we could lock the door and speed straight through this town. Endport's main street, designed by convict architects and built of local stone, according to the strictest classical principles, seemed slightly asymmetrical. Dotted in between the government buildings were simpler versions of what was fashionable in rural England two centuries ago: little four-room cottages with low doorways, built close to the street; their windows sometimes still barred against bushrangers and Aboriginal raiding parties. There was a gift shop in the prison warden's cottage. A painted wheelbarrow sat outside, full of miniature lavender. His sitting room was the main display area; the mantelpiece now showing off plastic ball-and-chain key rings, and little chocolates marketed as koala turds.

I slunk lower. "Someone is still calling me and hanging up."

Thomas took a deep breath. "Prank-calling teachers is practically on the syllabus."

"I'm getting scared."

He was silent a moment too long. "Don't be." He reached for my hand. "Don't be scared, Kate. You're in no danger."

Out the car window, people moved as if in their own dream. This town was an experiment in slow motion—a man waved to his friend like a character in an old flipbook; the friend stopped still, returning the greeting only as an afterthought. We passed the thrift store House of Welcome, with its hand-painted sign, fastened to the window: "Closing Down." No danger left there. We passed Carnival Take Away, where two girls, with beards of acne, were frying food, while outside, teenagers sat on the concrete pavement, eating their 2 P.M. dinner of fish and chips. Was that safe too? Would I be safe on the foreshore covered in tea tree? Or down the cliff, by the sand and rocks and sea? We passed the pier. The fishing boats' masts were swaying in the wind, their anchor chains sounding like bells. "I wouldn't swim in this crappy place if I was a fish."

"But you're a smart fish." He took a deep breath. "You've made a mark on me, Miss Byrne. You've certainly made your mark."

I stared straight ahead. "Will you keep Lucien in my class if she's found out?"

"Do me a favor. Go to work this afternoon and teach your class."

"And then what?"

"How old are you?"

"Twenty-two."

He parked down a dirt side road, around the corner from the primary school. "And then twenty-three, and twenty-four, and twenty-five, and you'll have more adventures." He took a deep breath. "It would seem you're growing up, my friend."

"No, I'm not."

He said nothing. I started to get out of the car without any kiss or fond words. This was the time to prove I didn't have separation anxiety; that I didn't care he was driving back to his real life. "Give me your little mouth," Thomas said, reaching for me. "I need your little mouth."

"No." I slammed the door and gave a Girl Guide salute. All along through the tea tree it sounded like a playground. Wattle birds seesawed, high note, then low note. Bright lorrikeets giggled like girls playing tiggy; and magpies, slightly awkward in black-and-white choir gowns, warbled their madrigals with gusto. I walked a few paces, then turning, watched the car drive away. *Wait!* I wanted to run after it. *Wait for me, I don't want to go to school! Can't I stay home and watch television?* Dust was rising from behind the wheels. I was standing still, and then I had to run in the opposite direction, because *I'm a naughty girl, late for school.*

I SAW THE PRIMARY school, the red brick building with its network of portable classrooms, and ran out of breath. It was dread winding me, not this sudden burst of exercise. Stumbling briskly through the empty playground, I passed wobbly hopscotch grids drawn over the concrete in colored chalk. Seagulls were milling around the Lilliputian drinking fountains and bins full of rejected lunches, holding court. The birds glared at me. I felt certain I was in trouble.

I'd only been out of Teacher's College for a few months when I first started working at Endport Primary School. It had seemed a good idea to take the job, just for a year, while I figured out if teaching was really what I wanted to do. On the first day of class, I got the kids to reorganize their desks in an unconventional configuration. When I called the roll I'd ask them, instead of just answering "Here," to call out their favorite food, or favorite hobby: a way of us all getting to know each other better. During creative exercises I'd encourage them to forget about spelling, to express themselves. Then, I would find myself standing before them, reading aloud a story about a nine-year-old girl who'd vomited "so, so, so much" that there were pyramids of vomit; all the seven wonders were re-created in bile, until eventually, this triumphant bulimic had her own entry in *The Guinness Book of Records.*

It was no wonder, under these conditions, that I fell into adultery. One afternoon, a month after I started, Thomas appeared at my classroom door looking for his son. It was some kind of destiny: a baby-sitter had already collected Lucien. Thomas drove me home instead. The following week, he made a very similar mistake and I asked if he'd like to come inside for a cool drink. I scurried around, kicking dirty laundry under the couch. Would he want to kiss me? I'd read an article on the merits of having an affair with an older man. A woman wrote about her lover always beating her friends at Trivial Pursuit; the benefits of napping in the afternoon.

Thomas did want to kiss me and the liaison conformed to my sense of what teachers ought to do. In high school I'd swapped long notes with my best friend speculating as to the sexual intrigues amongst the staff. Oh, the orgiastic world of adults: at the center of our fantasy was the ruddy sports teacher, who delighted in confiscating miscolored ribbons or stray jewelry. We found the harshest disciplinarians to be also the most libidinous—*Miss Morgan really requested long service leave, after her sex change, because Miss Longley had started going behind her back with Mrs. Gay Hardacre, from front office, thus proving my suspicion the sports department is going downhill.* Understanding our teachers' frustrations helped my friend and I, both still virgins, feel more kindly toward these people trading in petty humiliations.

Finally, I lurched through the door of my classroom. It was an aluminum portable with canvas blinds and fifteen nine-year-olds, holding a boisterous session of crayon-wielding wrestling. I fiddled with my skirt, still twisted from running, and praised the God of small-time floozies: the unsupervised children hadn't attracted the principal's attention. "Okay!" I clapped my hands. "I want everyone sitting down before I count to three. *One* . . ." A skirmish, purely melodramatic, began of *Oh-oh-oh! Get to the chair quickly!* My desk was at the front of the room. The children's desks occupied the middle, and along the back wall was a silent-reading area with bean-bags; bookshelves; a cardboard mailbox, where kids deposited notes to each other; and a "self-portrait wing" consisting of a low hanging mirror, beneath which the children sat and drew.

"*Two* . . ." Behind me, my teacher handwriting, all kink-less vowels and chubby consonants, spread like white lies over the blackboard. I could feel the sex still in my body; the more decorously I behaved, the more blatant its presence. At least I looked only mildly disheveled compared to these casualties: some had sweaty hair stuck to their foreheads from playing tiggy; bits of tanbark hung from their clothes.

"*Two and a half* . . ." Our studies related to endangered species. The endangered birds' names now sounded like love-talk: come to me my *buff-breasted button quail*, come to me my *crested shrike tit* and do what you do so well. Oh, you're my *helmeted honeyeater*, my big *regent honeyeater*. Yes! my *swift parrot*, my *night parrot!* . . . I never really meant to become a primary-school teacher. After leaving high school I started an arts degree. I had minors in a range of employer-unfriendly areas, and approaching graduation there seemed like absolutely nothing I wanted to do. I switched to Teacher's College, because I did enjoy baby-sitting. I really liked children. I liked the things children said when they grew candid. A three-year-old asks her five-year-old sister, "Can I join your burp club?" and this sophisticate answers, "No, I've closed it down." I liked reading children their stories. And I liked the stories: dogs and cats had magic powers; nasty people suffered slapstick doom. The world seemed manageable, its scale of anarchy to my liking. By becoming a teacher, it was like crossing to the other side. The staff room had the air of a bunker in a strife-torn, foreign land; the teachers, each morning, offered around mugs of some herbal tranquilizer, and I took tiny sips feeling like a spy.

"*Three!*" The children sat at their sloped wooden desks, the surfaces of which had long ago been carved up with initials. The fan was spinning, lazily, above. I checked the clock again. "Well done." There were still some busy whisperers. "Billy and Lucien, are you concentrating on your work?"

The two boys looked up sheepishly. They didn't really get along. Billy was the most popular boy in the class. Sandy-haired and reasonable, he was considered the voice of moral authority, having earned this status through his prowess at sport. I gazed at him sternly then turned to Lucien for the old double take: he was a replica of his father. He had the same beautiful face, which he could wear completely blank, adopting a slightly curled lip. He had a grave adult stare as if, in Saint-Exupéry's litmus test, he'd just seen a hat rather than the boa ingesting an elephant. Lucien, like Thomas before him, considered the other children to be profoundly stupid, and spent most of his lunchtimes with a book.

"So you really like reading?" I'd remarked at the beginning of the year. For a moment Lucien had looked at me with sympathy. I'd repeated the question. "Oh, I'm sorry," he'd answered politely, "I thought you asked, 'You really like breathing?'" I may as well have. He was the most erudite nine-year-old I had ever met. Talking to Lucien one forgot his age. He was a little conquistador stockpiling knowledge, and my class had been thrown into much turmoil due to his theories on everything from portraiture to the nonexistence of God. The publicity surrounding *Murder at Black Swan Point* could have explained his lack of faith. It conferred celebrity, which also came from being a city kid; however, his classmates parroted their parents' opinions of the book, most of which were decidedly uncomplimentary. It was fair to say when Mrs. Marne's true crime story was published, a lot of people felt very surprised. A lot of people also felt very betrayed: "Why couldn't she let the dead rest?" was the general sentiment, or more specifically, "She's opened up a Pandora's floodgate of worms!"

It became important for me to find invisible ways to protect Lucien. He was very good at drawing, something that gave him some status in the classroom, and it was mainly for his benefit I'd set up the self-portrait wing. Lucien would sit down and draw himself as Frankenstein's monster with pins in his head and blood dripping from his temples. "No, no, no, you're so handsome, this is silly," I'd said the first time. Not wanting to draw more attention to him, I hadn't really known what else to do. Lucien had continued in the same morbid vein: he'd draw himself with no eyes, a bird flying off, dangling his optical nerve in its claw; he'd draw himself with a bullet in his forehead and his tongue lolling. When finally, desperate, I'd told Thomas of this, he'd seemed bemused, as if Lucien were only doing it to gain my attention.

I thought there was another reason. What it meant for this child *psychically*, to have a mother obsessed with death and gore, I could only speculate. One day during crafts, Lucien had made a dream catcher, a contraption of net and feathers you hang from your bed as protection against bad dreams. He'd told me he wanted to give it to his mother. Then, on Mother's Day he'd drawn a picture of Veronica at work. She was perched over a wobbly keyboard which was stacked with enormous misshapen keys, like a mouth of dreadful teeth. Various suspicious images were surrounding her. "What are these?" I'd asked Lucien. "They're photographs of the houses in the murder," he'd said plainly. In each one was a bloodied body in a still more gruesome pose.

"How much does Lucien know about Veronica's book?" I'd asked Thomas.

"Well," he'd answered, "his mother tries to demystify things. We both think that's best. He knows a soul leaves a dead body, et cetera . . . I mean, there's no point treating Lucien as if he's a little half-wit. We've always spoken to him like to a short adult."

Under the subheading PROBLEMS, Lucien was now writing about our unfortunate koala population and their various diseases. "Very good, Lucien." He made a steeple with his fingers on which to rest his chin. His blazer was hanging on the back of his chair. "That's very interesting." Next door, Billy was writing about the northern hairy-nosed wombat: *Wombats generally eat plants. A wombat never eats meat. Wom-*

bats can break into farms and damage farm animals' legs. It was like a syllogism gone wrong: my favorite thing about these reports was just how badly they'd been cribbed from any source the kids could find. I was watching plagiarism in its rawest form; how could a wombat, a forty-centimeter-high wombat, break into a farm and kneecap all the animals? Who'd have suspected this creature, so seemingly earnest, was the thug of the animal world? "Good boy, Billy." The point was for them to gain more confidence in their research skills.

I walked around the classroom reading the other reports. Despite horrible stories about starving echidnas and obese possums, it was really the human condition on display here. Darren would proudly acknowledge his position as the class bully. He was in a codependent relationship with Alastair, his main victim, a fleshy boy who was deeply unintelligent. (In Alastair's astounding sentences—a shantytown of corrugated words—the child described the endangered Leadbetter possum, claiming as one problem: *my dad runs over them all the time*.) Alastair accepted Darren's lack of respect with teary fatalism. But to make matters worse, he had an unrequited crush on Danielle, a little gap-toothed Aryan.

Danielle was now describing, without much empathy, the fate of the Forester kangaroo, hunted into near extinction down here. She sat next to Eliza, a businesslike child, small for her age, with a blunt-cut orange fringe. Eliza had done a project on the Tasmanian tiger. Past and present tenses merged; it was unclear whether the animal was endangered or extinct. PROBLEMS: *People shot all the Tasmanian tigers because they ate their chickens*. SOLUTIONS: *If anyone ever finds any tigers they should be put in a zoo.* REFERENCES: *We used a* World Book Encyclopedia. *We couldn't find out much about it in the* World Book Encyclopedia.

Someone cleared his throat. It was Henry Ledder, a blue-eyed boy with curly dark hair. He had a scribble of red marker on his neck from a lunchtime pen war. "What do you do if you've finished?"

"Those of you who've finished might like to draw yourselves with your endangered species."

At their desks were old yogurt containers full of stubby crayons and pencils. Henry drew himself eating cake with a honey possum. Next to him, Anaminka, a quiet thoughtful girl, drew herself dressed in her pajamas standing by a tree of night parrots. When my fourth-graders first started working on endangered species, all the children chose pretty birds, and the girls cried because the tiger reminded them of their Labradors. They didn't think it was fair: it wasn't fair that all these animals were dying out, or had died out. Supposedly this was a moral breakthrough: before the age of, say, eight, traditionalists claim experiences are really only understood as unfair if the child himself is somehow disadvantaged. *Q. What isn't fair? A. Telling them where the donkey's tail is at my birthday party.* Apparently only later can they see things from another person's point of view. *Q. What isn't fair? A. If someone crashes his bicycle and dies.*

Perhaps people confused a savagery in children's responses for a lack of moral depth. What the children hadn't learned to do was to modulate, or translate, their thoughts into the refined, socially coded answers of adults. It was true their moral logic was occasionally skewed, but their opinions were still considered. And I wanted to know what they thought the difference was between right and wrong. Despite our initial hiccup, examining the metaphysics of local history, it seemed a good idea to get the children thinking further about ideals of truth and justice. I found a cartoon of Plato, and explained that he was a man who believed in an invisible world where everything existing on Earth was in its perfect form. "What if we lived in a world where everyone told the truth?" I asked my class. "Can you always know truth?"

> Anaminka: *You need research to find out, but some things are impossible to research.*
> Eliza: *You can't research God.*
> Anaminka: *You can't research bacteria at this age.*
> Billy: *But if everyone tells the truth, you could talk up to the sky and say [putting on a deep voice], "God, are you real?" and he'd have to tell you.*
> Henry [pretending to be God]: *"G'day!"*
> Lucien: *But how would you know if that was the truth?*
> Billy: *Because everyone told the truth.*
> Lucien: *But how do you know if everyone was telling the truth?*
> Billy: *Because that was the truth.*
> Lucien: *But how would you know?*

Lucien had made it clear he disagreed with most of what was being said. Finally I called on him to share his impressions. As usual there was a mind-spinning adultness to his speech, and then a strangeness as it slid back into nine-year-old patois. I was ready to find his pretensions endearing, but the depth of his ideas left me and the others near speechless.

> Lucien: *About seven thousand years ago everybody knew that the Earth was the center of the universe. Now it's not true. It was true then, but it isn't now. So my point is you can change the truth. But it usually happens after years . . . Truth is a flexible substance.*

There was a knock on the classroom door. All the children looked up to see the principal standing outside. Lillian Hurnell, neat in her tweed suit, wore so much foundation she glowed orange. I rushed to let her in, asking, "Children, how do we greet a guest?"

"Good afternoon, Miss Hurnell."

"Good afternoon, 4B." She turned to me. "Miss Byrne, may I have a brief word?"

"Certainly." I followed her to the door. Lillian was from the equivalent of Tasmanian royalty; her family settled very early and their dessert spoons and embroidered christening dresses had been donated to the town's museum. Her family homestead had bluestone walls. And one wall was papered with pages from an old *Woman's Weekly*. My mother had told me Lillian's aunt became pregnant to a farmhand and the young woman shot herself. The Hurnells covered the stained bluestone with pretty pictures.

Lillian stepped outside. "I was just checking you were all right."

"Yes, fine."

"Elsbeth saw you limping back late from lunch."

"Oh! I had a doctor's appointment."

"You do look flushed," Lillian agreed.

"A little fever. Thank goodness I can spend the weekend sleeping. By Monday I'll be fine." I paused. "Luckily the children all seem to be in perfect health." I turned and saw, through the window, each child's face staring back at me. "They're all doing really well."

Lillian, having followed my gaze, became self-conscious. "Right, I'd better let you get back to it then."

"Thanks for the concern, Lillian." I nodded gravely. "It's appreciated."

"Kate?"

I turned, holding the door handle. "Yes?"

"There's a snag in your panty hose."

"Oh dear, Lillian." I smiled. "I'm so glad you noticed."

I closed the door, confident that Lillian was offended by no more than my lack of grooming and punctuality. I continued checking the children's work: Eliza colored in an earnest tiger; Billy, a loglike wombat. I stood still, watching them draw. It was amazing how their skills advanced: at approximately thirteen months, infants grab pencils with their fists to spread scribble all over anything; around the age of three, children start drawing spirals or circles as if putting to paper their memory of floating; then the circle becomes a head, and arms and legs are fastened, like sunbeams radiating off the sun. These children, now, took up their colored pencils and they seemed so assured. Each line bore no trace of doubt or ambivalence. They believed their drawings to be straightforward, and they were: like the beautiful maps to some lost world.

The only child whose pictures made me worry was Lucien. He had drawn a family of blind koalas, all hanging limp from a tree. Koalas apparently suffered from skin cancer, morphological abnormalities due to inbreeding, and chlamydia, which led to blindness and infertility. Ninety percent of the population had died in the last ten years. *President Clinton has been written to about this,* Lucien claimed. *We need his help to write the National Koala Act.* He was diligently drawing himself with hulking shoulders, and a square, robotlike upper body. Hopefully, he thought chlamydia came from too much sun. Bolted across his arm he drew a large water pistol. "Lucien," I asked, "you're not going to hurt the koala, are you?"

"*Nooo,*" he said, "I'm protecting it."

"Oh, so you're, like, on the same team?"

He rolled his eyes. "Yep."

"Very good, Lucien. Well done."

Once I'd asked Thomas, "Do you worry about your son's education now that we're lovers?" "On the contrary," he'd claimed. "You're being far more attentive, far more tender to my son." He'd taken a deep breath. "In fact, I'm only doing this for his education." I had balked. "No really, he's flesh of my flesh. You'll see him. You'll see him first thing in the morning. You'll see him when he leaves. You'll stroke his hair and think of me, and he'll have no idea."

I looked out the window. Slowly, the mothers were gathering in the playground. There was an old ship's bell under the jacaranda. In five minutes, at half past three, it would ring and all the children would run outside. I loved the way they fell out the classroom door, as if being disgorged by a sea monster;

then, the theater of matching them to their mothers—the blond to the brunette, the charismatic to the deeply dopey. All these glaze-eyed, drowsy kids would suddenly be sharp as lawyers, doing deals on sleepovers. They would run to dump their schoolbags, before showing off on the monkey bars.

I moved around the room trying to seem natural and bright to those on the other side of the glass. Most of the mothers wore sneakers and track pants. They had sensible hair and sensible shoes. Except for Veronica. Pale Veronica with skin that held the light. Through the window, I'd long studied her looks; her trademark red lipstick confusing, or perhaps accentuating, all the orchid delicacy she had going for her. She reminded me of the prettiest girl at any party. She walked with a perfectly blank expression until she saw someone she liked—one of the vaguely comme il faut mothers—whom she might greet extravagantly. She'd guiltily smoke the other's cigarettes, tilting her head, baring a long smooth neck as she exhaled. As soon as the bell rang, she'd stamp out her butt and offer around the mints from the glove box.

I turned back to the class, but it was difficult to muster composure. I had not expected to see her. I'd thought she'd be away for the weekend, but the vigilante on about the ethics of journalism had driven her back. I wiped clean the black-board, while sizing up her physical strength. If it came down to some sort of tussle, I would obviously have the advantage of youth; she was pushing forty and I was at least fifteen years her junior. Plus she was so thin, very thin and graceful; if I wasn't badly stunned I could easily outbulk her.

Veronica's main advantage would be strategy. Ever since

she was young she'd read these parlor detective stories where crime is so pristine, always conforming to a trusted formula: after the stableboy-with-ringworm finds the deceased under a pile of hay, everything is conducted in a most urbane fashion; interrogations take place during high tea. When the murderer breaks down and politely confesses, they all have gin and tonics on the lawn.

One day Veronica had had *I-could-do-that* syndrome. Always canny, she discovered true crime sold better than fiction—and who could make this stuff up? A small-town American football star murders local girls using soda pop bottles. A wealthy British doctor kills his wife and her maid; then cuts off their identifying characteristics: fingertips, eyeballs (the maid had a bad squint), and teeth (his wife's were bucked). By this stage Veronica was thirty-five. She was married to a lawyer, with one young child and, even though it was inappropriate for me to speculate, perhaps the marriage wasn't going so well. Black Swan Point's story was attractive because it was classic: nice upper-middle-class girl meets nice upper-middle-class boy. They marry young. They have trouble communicating. They have three babies in a row, and she gets fat. He starts fucking a pretty young employee. She gets more desperate. Most often this story ends with years and years of passive-aggression, or with the now middle-aged nice girl getting screwed over as her husband starts another family. This figure, Margot Harvey, had broken out of the mold, and went blazing into the night, howling, *"No! No! I will not be civilized about being replaced! I will not retire gracefully!"*

"Okay, kids." I clapped my hands. "It's time to clean up.

Quietly!" There was the scrape of their chairs as they all jumped up; then the fiddly business of packing one's pencil case. Watching them prepare to leave made me the tiniest bit sad. "This weekend, as homework, I want you to finish your drawings." They stuffed their pictures into their schoolbags. Then the bell rang, and soon their mothers were all standing in the doorway, helping to retrieve lost lunchboxes.

Out the window Veronica stood alone.

When *Murder at Black Swan Point* first came out I had been stunned. She and I were initially quite cordial, but after reading her book, I walked around my house as if visible from every angle; suddenly the walls were made of eyes. Like some primitive version of hell, every vase knew I was bad. Abruptly Veronica stopped waving in the mornings. She stopped entering the classroom. Then, at night, late, the telephone started ringing. My evenings were so silent that the sound could startle me at the best of times. I would answer and often there was a low rumble in the background. If it were just children, why were they still awake? The call was coming from a public place. At first I would hang up, but later I became more brazen; I'd stay on the line, waiting. To prove I wasn't scared I would stay there, hoping someone might speak.

I watched Lucien as he crept from the room, walking toward his mother—"When he says something smart you'll be proud. When he mispronounces a word, you'll be touched. When he's crabby, when he yawns, when he laughs you'll watch him, but you'll see me." Veronica quickly took her son's bag and ushered him to the sleek silver car I'd traveled in only hours before. They drove away and I turned from the window, suddenly alone. All the other children had stormed outside.

These Friday afternoons had the air of a one-sided game of hide-and-seek. The playground, the toilet cubicles, the locker rooms all appeared to be empty, but rather than searching out clever nooks and crannies, I'd count to twenty and walk—slightly too briskly—through the Cyclone wire gates. Quietly, I closed the classroom door. I bent to lock it, and a shudder ran through me. In the door's olive paint-work, two words were now scratched in a maniac's hand: *I KNOW.*

Kitty spied the stainless steel instruments.

I'm scared," *whispered Kitty Koala, peek-peeking through the window. Between her splayed paws, Kitty spied a naked fluorescent bulb illuminating stainless steel instruments, a shining metal trolley, and a refrigerator. The mortuary room of any country hospital, she realized, was bound to be minimal. Two policemen, a crime-scene photographer, a technical assistant, and the doctor performing the postmortem hovered about the drab room. Finally the doctor gave his assistant a nod. The metal trol-*

ley was wheeled over to the fridge, Ellie's naked, blood-smeared body transferred.

"Oh sweet Jesus!" the doctor appeared to groan, surveying the horrific wounds.

The men spoke sadly amongst themselves. Kitty strained to understand what they were saying. After all these years she still found broader Australian accents difficult to interpret. It has been suggested that Australians' pronunciation is due to a prevalent nose inflammation, caused by pollen in the air. Others say that a dry climate causes thinner mucous tissues in the nasal cavities, producing a harsher quality of voice. Kitty believed it to be mere lip laziness; "The Australian often speaks without obviously opening his lips at all," she complained, "through an immobile slit, and in extreme cases through closed teeth."

"Oh well," reckoned Kitty, "the crime's brutality speaks for itself."

The men considered the girl's every pore from every angle. It was always sad when a young person passed away, especially in such brutal circumstances. Kitty felt herself start to blush. Perhaps these men couldn't help thinking of the petit *dalliances they'd kept from their own wives, the trysts at conferences, the one-night stand on a hot night, late, legs spread ... Oh dear! The lowermost parts of Ellie's body were now a purplish red from postmortem lividity. The killer must have found the girl asleep in her room, and started the attack while she was prone. It made the bear so glum: Ellie had been stabbed repeatedly in the chest and abdomen. At this point she had presumably woken and tried to defend herself; her hands and calves bore knife marks, traces of attempts to both push and kick her attacker away.*

After Ellie's chest was examined for rib fractures, a thoracic-abdominal incision was made from shoulder to shoulder, crossing down over the breasts. Goodness! Kitty found it hard to keep up with all the doctor's procedures. It made her dizzy as next the ribs and the cartilage were cut through to expose the heart and lungs. Then, the heart, lungs, esophagus, and trachea were removed en bloc; each organ was weighed, its external surface examined.

She sighed. On and on the postmortem went, until eventually, the assistant put all Ellie's organs into garbage bags to prevent seepage. While he sewed the bags inside the body, Kitty scratched her furry head, deep in thought. It was unusual for a crime of passion to turn into such a brutal case of mutilation. Whoever had killed Ellie wanted to eradicate the girl's physical beauty even in death. And another thing was certain, the koala realized: the murderer was strong to gouge such deep cuts.

STILL SHAKING, I locked myself inside my car and just started driving. I had visited Black Swan Point before. I knew that the Georgian buildings turned into brown brick houses; that empty play equipment in people's yards looked like lost children metamorphosed. Rural Australia was full of perfectly tended ghost towns: a war memorial, bearing all the same family names, stood surrounded by stumpy rose bushes. Each bush had been too lovingly pruned or else stunted by this heat, heat that sits on your shoulders. Three teenage boys rode up and down the main street on their mountain bikes. When they saw me they wouldn't meet my eye; they raised first their arses, then their front wheels into the air; colts proving they could buck. And just on the outskirts of the town, yellow road signs warning of schoolchildren and kangaroos had been shot full of bullet holes. The kangaroos, their paws held up in rigor mortis, lay like forgotten crime victims by the edge of the road. Pray for rain to wash it all away. Imagine feeling like you're living at the very end of the earth, and also knowing that you are.

Nearby was the street where Ellie Siddell had lived in the year before her death. "We don't like that road," a local woman had told me. "We call it Murder Road." Murder

Road was long and thin. You started off on high land then descended down a dusty dirt track until you hit her family's house. People said if it were their daughter they would've hired a bulldozer. The house was very plain and symmetrical, with a wide veranda and one little window set high up: I had decided that was the window of her bedroom. It must have had a slanting roof.

The crime photographs in Lucien's careful drawing were included in his mother's book. What was uncanny was how familiar each interior seemed. The living room had every era of sturdy furniture represented: squat armchairs upholstered in autumnal fabric; a sound system the size of a couch; an oak dining table with thick, carved legs; and one painting—a landscape. The bathroom, fitted with postwar amenities, had a basin with square lines in the mint green of Australian art deco. The kitchen had a frill of gingham curtain over each window; and high stools surrounded the aging linoleum benches. Did she sit on these kitchen stools, her feet not reaching the floor, feeling incredibly grown up? At dinner parties did she squash peas into the table's crevices before taking flirty sips from the avuncular guest's wineglass?

Since none of Ellie's family or close friends had spoken to Veronica one had to read between the lines. This was what I imagined: on family drives to the Black Swan Point house, Ellie would deep-breathe on the window, then, in the fogged-up glass, draw pictures of women with pronounced erogenous zones. She'd fall asleep in the car and have to be carried to bed. And in the morning, wearing plastic gold Barbie slippers, she'd tiptoe down the gnarled driftwood steps onto the sand. All the boys were on old surfboards, paddling out to the sandbank. The littlest boy paddled with a rake, dipping the stick end in the water, then the fingers; just moving round in circles. She was one of the girls with skinny legs doing synchronized swimming in the shallows; she and her cousins collected jellyfish in buckets and buried each other in the sand. They were being protected from bad things so strenuously that the slightest irregularity—like the tattooed woman once seen bathing—could overwhelm. Or else it could underwhelm: walking her new puppy along the shore Ellie let a man pat the dog. He asked her if she ever put her hands in her underpants at night. "No, how silly!" she told him laughing, dragging the dog away.

Ellie attended a private school in Hobart, where girls sang the same hymns their mothers had sung. On the oval she did stretching exercises with her class. The girls leaned back. The sky seemed a most daring blue. A violin, like a rusting swing, sounded from an open window in the music school. They leaned to the right, their ponytails synchronized. The French mistress in her academic gown walked her two tiny dogs around the oval, her finger conducting the music. Was she searching for smokers behind the art room? Could dogs develop gout? Would she rile the gym teacher by calling imperiously, "Young ladies do not run!" The gym teacher, an enormous woman with red nose and cheeks, defined the word *ruddy*. She wore tracksuit pants instead of a tennis skirt, which was just as well. There'd been hilarity when, demonstrating how to hurdle, she'd lifted up her leg, revealing dark pubic hair crawling halfway down her thigh. "Show us again, show us again!" cried an elfin bad girl, with buckteeth and a pageboy haircut. "Could you please show us how to hurdle one more time?"

Ellie was not a bad girl: a girl whom the flute teacher, with his dirty turtleneck, might ogle. Those girls hitched up their skirts on the lawn, during lunchtime, to work on their tans. It seemed they understood the secrets of alchemy, but weren't telling. With their neat bodies, they'd rise at the bell linking arms as if, lightheaded, they had to lean on their best friends' shoulders. They realized history only happened in textbooks, and read magazines behind their Bunsen burners. Nothing would really go wrong—the worst thing was when a girl's father died of cancer, but everyone took the afternoon off school, and at the funeral clutched each other, all weeping more vigorously than any team of widows—girls with lovely upbringings who don't understand disaster.

Standing in the locker room, pungent with sneakers and spray deodorant, the bad girls whispered loudly about boys. The film in Science, explaining there was no bone in the penis, had not surprised them. Neither had the slide show, organized by the school nurses, which demonstrated in passing that an erection did not jut out of a man's body, horizontally, at a ninety-degree angle. All Ellie's friends were reaching for their protractors, amazed. But the bad girls smirked. The way they'd smirked when the nurse came to class and put a tampon in a glass of water. They stripped off their gym uniforms brazenly, showing off flat, tanned stomachs. But Ellie dressed and undressed so no one could see this new body she didn't know what to do with: put your track pants on under your school dress; unbutton your dress; put your gym shirt on over the dress; pull the dress down.

Still, you could never guard against the shock of seeing a newly developed breast. The first girls to develop were, naturally, sluts. But if the breasts came at the right time you could be extremely popular. The worst fate was a "pyramid tit," something conical, and frankly ineffectual, in its shiny white trainer bra.

After graduating, most of Ellie's friends moved from Tasmania onto the mainland. She just wanted to leave home. She'd grown up in the most beautiful house in Battery Point. Walking up the road she could smell the flowers, great fleshy camellias, spilling over the fence. The ceilings rose high above her and below were wide floorboards of Huon pine from the rain forest. Cedar, resembling mahogany, had been transported from New South Wales for mantelpieces and joinery. Every chair had been exquisitely turned. Each painting was another new town's violet sunset. Eleanor Siddell had been loved to the gills. But in Hobart she knew every street intimately: all the stories of every corner, and of all the people in all the houses. Hobart was probably the most stunning city in the world. Boats came up the wide blue Derwent and docked right in its center. From her window she counted each white sail, remembering a Grimm's fairy tale her grandfather had read to her, "The Prince Afraid of Nothing"; "Once upon a time there was a prince who had got tired of living in his father's house, and as he was afraid of nothing he thought: I'll go out into the wide world and I'll see plenty of strange sights."

She moved to the peninsula, and started her new life working for the vet. She went to the supermarket by herself. She bought food with the money she'd earned. She took the grocery bags to the car thinking, The girls from school should see me now. I am the last person they'd expect to have a lover. *Lover*: even the word sounded so adult, straight from a movie. And she was the star, running back to her job with dried semen between her legs. Just the thought of his mouth on top of her mouth was thrilling. When they'd writhe, she'd think, We're two sticks trying to make fire. She wanted to learn everything straightaway. Teach me all the little tricks to fucking. How do people do this great, big sex thing? I want to get good at it, quickly. What should my face look like? Was that too loud? What do I do with my hands? It was strange to have all this delicious attention, for him to touch her and for that alone to make him shiver. Had he made some mistake? The struck-dumbness he affected every time she undressed and lay on the bed; all his sighing and eyes rolled back—was someone beautiful standing behind her? Everyone should have one great secret to carry round as a talisman. Then, when people look at you, thinking *she's like this*, or *she's only this*, they'll always be wrong.

I sat in my car outside the Siddells' house. The aftermath of the girl's murder was nightmarish for her parents. After it became clear an outsider wasn't responsible, some local people felt Ellie had brought this on herself through recklessness. She had done the wrong thing and justice had been savage.

When Veronica Marne tried to investigate the twelve-year-old crime as a local, her neighbors were tight-lipped. The old story kept coming to the fore: no one could believe Margot Harvey capable of such a brutal crime. She was an incredibly kind woman, practical and generous. If someone was having a hard time and needed help with their kids, she'd organize people to take the children for a few hours after school. If someone were sick, she'd prepare food. In newspapers, after any unexpected disaster, people stand around, a fist to the air, howling: *Why this town!* It was the same at Black Swan Point. *This is a quiet place*, people said. *This is a good quiet place, we don't even lock our doors.*

No car was now in the house's driveway, but the lawn was freshly mowed and a bird feeder full of seed. The curtains were drawn, although I felt I'd already seen inside: Ellie's bedroom, according to the crime photos, was incredibly messy. She had twin beds; one she slept in, one stacked with stuffed toys. Her clothes carpeted the floor. Lipsticks and perfumes were spread over each inch of the dressing table. On the wall were snapshots of her school friends: girls in dance dresses; all of them at school camp pulling spastic faces. It was hard to believe she'd brought her lover here, but she was still only nineteen. And I bet every time Graeme Harvey led her to the single bed, and pushed away a layer of debris, Ellie wished she'd remembered to tidy up. When first he stood in the doorway, and noticed the clothes and junk in such a mess all over her floor, I bet there was something in his expression which made her jump on him and kiss him wildly to divert his attention.

The police bagged nearly sixty items from the house, and over half came from off her bedroom floor: a pair of pink underpants; a sports bra; a T-shirt; a bathing costume; a facecloth; two towels; magazines; candy wrappers; tissues; more underwear; a nurse's uniform; a cigarette packet; a nightgown; a box of matches from The Sand and Waves Tudor Inn; a polyester Snoopy toy; a white tennis shoe; a pair of women's tracksuit pants . . . The list went on in excruciating detail, but also included brown matter labeled "blood scrapings"; samples of Ellie's blood, her hair, her nail and muscle tissue; scrapings from under her fingernails; and the knife found lying next to the body.

I started the car and drove away. I understood Ellie because I gave her my own story. I didn't understand Margot. She hadn't just killed the girl in a brief bout of madness, this supposedly meek woman had mutilated her enemy horribly. I turned out of Murder Road—and call it superstition, or a knock-on-wood—I proceeded toward the Suicide Cliffs.

The ride should have taken around twenty minutes, but I was driving my grandfather's old blue car: the biggest Mercedes-Benz ever made and you couldn't have paid anyone to take it off your hands. I drove slowly, and tried very hard to imagine what Margot would have been thinking. It was not as though *Murder at Black Swan Point* shed any light. Veronica had described this last drive in a style which swung between the melodramatic and the faux-clinical: *her* Mrs. Harvey slipped and slid all over the road, Ellie's blood still staining her hands. The woman had freed herself from a life spent in Goodness, and lit a cigarette with almost postcoital pleasure. But just as Veronica was really starting to enjoy herself, she pulled back out of respect for readers with less liberated sensibilities. The true-crime writer's ethical stance was inherently false—Veronica acted as an intermediary between evil and the reader, positioning herself as above reproach. But how could she get inside the criminal mind, while bending backward to then show her horror at the deed? In every chapter she'd tried to cloak her fascination as social responsibility. Her own perversion as research.

Suddenly, my car started making a strange, high-pitched whistling. I slowed down a little, hoping to calm the engine. The road was dirt. Pine telephone poles rose out of the dust, and as I drove further there were fewer signs of life. I passed farmhouses, long abandoned, collapsing under wild ivy: cottages with sunken verandas and broken windows. In each paddock, fence posts lay in the grass like old bones. A rusting bathtub functioned as a water trough, but only broken-down motors grazed in the sun. I'd heard it said that, long ago, when Port Arthur closed down, the convicts settled here, on the opposite side of the highway to the free settlers. The settlers had previously been given land grants and convict labor. Their descendants, now our community's rural gentry, still live behind their forefathers' hedgerows. Once when a man fell down drunk outside a grand neighbor's house, my mother watched the neighbor get a shovel and turn the man over to see if he was all right—noblesse oblige.

If Establishment Man and Establishment Woman were sold as action toys, the girl doll would come with a wardrobe of flat shoes and tartan skirts of unflattering length. Sold separately would be the old dictionary and gold pocket watch passed down from her Scottish paternal great-grandfather. For Establishment Man one could buy a set of golf clubs and some street signs named after a forebear. Tasmania's place-names gave a fine insight into our settlers' sensibilities. Wander around the game board from Cape Grim to the Never Never to Nameless Lake, perhaps skip Sympathy Hills, head toward the Suicide Cliffs and dine at Purgatory Hill, or more likely the Devil's Kitchen.

Margot Harvey was born, just after World War II, into a respectable Tasmanian family with good Christian values. Margot, I'm sure, would have been encouraged to be a nice girl, not too clever, not too opinionated. She'd have grown up wearing hats and gloves wherever she went; and, like my mother, might not have heard anyone utter the word *shit* until she was in her twenties. Tasmanians held fast to colonial decorum, and Hobart was a small town. Everyone knew everyone else; everyone knew what everyone else was doing. *Be a good girl.* There was a keen sense of right and wrong. Margot would be a good girl, so she would be safe.

From my grandparents' bookshelves and from gossamer, I had tried to cobble a picture of her: before bed my Margot read an English story about *Mrs. Do-As-You-Would-Be-Done-By* and *Mrs. Be-Done-By-As-You-Did*. Other children borrowed better books from the library—one fiction, if two nonfictions were also read. She was not allowed to borrow books; her mother thought she might catch tuberculosis. Once her father bought her a beautifully bound set of Dickens from an estate sale, and her mother gave him a real dressing-down because of the potential for germs. All the books were left out in the sun for the day before she was permitted to even look at them. Later, in boarding school, the girls drank coffee made from the water in their hot-water bottles, and read under the blankets with torches. Some of the girls got into each other's beds. One girl was said to use the new plastic wrap on her fingers; she claimed it was hygienic. Margot willed herself to sleep. Some girls climbed out the window to smoke with boys in the lane. If they got into trouble they'd leave school, and maybe come back the next year. Margot would stay asleep and she would get everything she deserved.

What *Murder at Black Swan Point* left unmentioned was that Margot's parents had divorced: Margot's father had abandoned her mother. None of the other girls at school had divorced parents. No one else had a stepmother who was an adulteress. In the wood-paneled dining hall, as Margot's classmates tried to converse in French, she stared down at her table setting. She'd always presumed the knife and fork were married, and the spoon was their daughter. Now she realized the knife and spoon weren't family, they were actually lying on the linen serviette having an affair. That was why the fork, on the other side of the place mat, was always fuming, alone. People crossed over the road so as not to speak to Margot's mother, the divorcée who was always crying. Margot wanted to pick up her fork and throw it through the window. She had to concentrate all her energy not to do the bad thing. And in that second, the whole scene played out: the shocked faces turning slowly toward her, the hot wash of shame. But *I've always been a good girl,* she thought, staying still. *Even reaching into this fruit bowl, I will pull out the bruised fruit.*

Margot sailed on the boat to London in 1966. She was twenty. She met a boy from home and they married three years later. Her main goal was to make her husband happy. After their second anniversary, the couple returned to Tasmania and they had a daughter. Hobart didn't agree with the young mother. Her husband worked long hours, and she was often left alone with the baby. Maybe she was worried this handsome man had a wandering eye. She gave birth to two more girls in the next four years, and later her family bought them a piece of land with a new farmhouse on Black Swan Point, two hours outside the city. She set to work decorating the house. (It was very much of its period, mid 1970s, low, brown-brick, and surrounded by casuarinas with spindly leaves, spider's legs, screening it from the street.) Graeme set up his veterinary practice. Things were going well. He employed a girl to take care of some secretarial work. And at first Margot thought Eleanor Siddell was sweet. She came from a similar background, but she was fifteen years younger, so it was a slightly different world, a slightly more permissive world that she had inherited. Ellie was full of life, a jumping jack of a girl. Sometimes Margot dropped the children at the veterinary clinic when there was shopping to be done. It was helpful Ellie was so good with her daughters. Ellie let them draw with the fluorescent markers. She let them lick the envelopes, or staple invoices. Sometimes, at home, the girls drew pictures of their friend with ribbons in her hair and frills on her skirts; with bow lips and dimples—all the twin-kling features of the cheapest plastic doll.

Try to be nice to that girl, she's away from her family, Margot thought. Try to be kind to that girl with her big, brown eyes. "She's oddly bovine," Margot told her husband, "with those big brown cow eyes." He just laughed. Graeme was working late and working early. Margot watched how he lied; how he modulated his voice before relaxing into the lie. He was smart. Rather than tensing up, he'd stretch out his shoulders as if to say, "I've nothing to hide." But Margot watched the way the girl gazed at him. She watched the way the girl swanned round, arching her back. Ellie blocked the sun. Had she grown up promising, "I will not marry a man who looks at me as though I'm drowned. Who starts staring at a girl with the top button of her shirt always open. Who probably tells her, like he once told me, *you're my beauty queen, you with the Ferris wheel eyes...*"

The Mercedes continued to whine. I didn't know this side of the highway very well, but people always joked there were a lot of village idiot types here, where I was about to break down. "It is a little inbred" was all my father would say discreetly. Some people in the hills had never even driven the two hours to Hobart. In the northwest of the state, only twenty years ago, if a small town knew a salesman was driving through, parents would apparently chain up their children, because these kids didn't have good road sense. Their ancestors had probably got caught for slapstick misdemeanors—they stole a roll of ribbon and it unraveled all the way home.

Smoke started rising from the car's bonnet and I remembered reading about a town in America which formed in the late nineteenth century around a psychiatric hospital. In the 1960s, a combination of funding cuts and liberalism led to all the patients being released, and now they all lived in the town with the unemployed hospital workers. Probably in the 1870s that was pretty much what it was like here, although divergent groups still coexisted today. The state's rally car speed tests were conducted upriver on the grounds of the local asylum. It was not as though the insane just observed from their cell windows. Apparently there were little circles of people outside. They were standing in their nightgowns, watching the cars speeding past, almost like human pylons.

My car was screeching. The smoke became thicker. I thought of Margot's headlights on high beam; the stolen cigarette and the road's white lines leading her on. The screeching became harsher still. I had to pull over, but when I tried to brake nothing happened. A blind corner loomed. I pumped the brakes. Nothing happened. The car only picked up speed. I screamed around the bend, scraping the side against the tea trees. I caught a flash of blue. A little postcard of bay. To my right there was a sheer drop. I pulled on the handbrake: nothing. The car sped down the hill and I stopped breathing. Swinging the wheel from side to side, I tried to slow the car. I tried to slow the car using a skiing motion, praying all the while no one would come speeding toward me. Further down, the road dipped. There was a patch of green. I drove straight toward it closing my eyes, flinching before I crashed into shrubbery.

Dark smoke rose from the bonnet. I sat hyperventilating, my hands still gripping the wheel. On the other side of the road, up a little way, a spatter-work chair was covered with bags of apples—people left their excess produce by the side of the road and other people stopped to pick up that produce, leaving money in the empty jam jar. I sat, unable to inhale enough oxygen, staring at the chair. Once when my parents took a bag of apples, forgetting to pay, they realized what they'd done and drove the half hour back, only to be told by the man at the orchard that since they'd been so honest he wouldn't dream of charging. *We live here because nasty things don't happen. We live here because people are good. We have home-made honey at the local store, and lovely bed-and-breakfasts.*

I put my head in my hands, howling. The smoke was dark gray. Throwing open the door I propelled myself into the undergrowth. I lay there, my mouth full of grass, waiting for the car to blow up. Then I just lay there. "If I buy a bag of apples, and I put one dollar fifty in the jar," I whispered finally, "please let the car be all right. Please let the car, and me, be all right." I stood up and walked toward the Mercedes. The smoke was thinning. Shaking, I took my handbag from the passenger seat. I took coins from my purse, put them in the jar, and walked back to the car with a bag of apples. Having fulfilled the terms of my contract, I locked the car door and turned away. I was in the middle of nowhere.

If I'd told my parents this was happening, they would have come speeding down, thrilled to be called, huffing and puffing with love and worry. When they arrived I'd have had to tell them the truth. "I can't do that," I whispered. "I can't do that to them." They'd have been heartbroken. Rather than taking me by the hair and calling me a little slut, there'd have been doleful glances and deep sighs. I was concerned for them enough already—their skin seemed thinner lately; they couldn't read cooking instructions without their glasses. In the winter, my father had written me a letter, claiming, "Life here is as it always has been, and never was. Battalions of ants are marching through the kitchen. Your mother and I are having trouble seeing them."

An apple in my hand, I started walking. Waves, slow but persistent, were not far off. They sounded like a huge animal drawing breath. I felt for my own pulse, but my hand trembled too much. A car was approaching. I darted into the bushes and silvereyes fluttered out of my way. Under the trees, the air was still. Every branch lying in my path wished no ill, nor any luck; and the dirt smelled rich with its own fertile plans. The car passed and I choked back a sob. Only hours ago someone had stood up and attacked Veronica for her lack of integrity. This must have been incredibly humiliating; as good a reason as any for turning psychotic. And on this curving road, it would have been impossible to tell if it was the Marnes' silver car, or a mechanically minded Samaritan, until the bumper was upon you.

I was dressed for a motel room, not the backcountry. Suddenly my knee-length skirt seemed too short, my heels a fraction high. Some people claimed that the day Margot Harvey cracked was the day she saw her husband and the girl together. People said Margot had started following him. One day she looked in a window and saw him with his lover. How would Lucien's mother have told her "short adult" about this? Of course, she'd have had to soften it a little; but children are potentially the true-crime novelist's ideal audience. Children understand tragedy in a way adults are unable to: atom by atom. Untainted by a hundred other learned horrors, they are haunted for the appropriate length of time. They ask a thousand unanswerable questions. The story stays with them; they dream of it. I kept walking under the trees, and I imagined *Murder at Black Swan Point*, a version for Lucien to read. A book for little clairvoyants which told the truth.

· MURDER AT BLACK SWAN POINT ·

"That old pussycat's seen it all."

Terence Tiger reckoned Missy Pink-Princess, the gregarious three-legged tabby who roamed the peninsula's hotels, could well have witnessed something crucial. Sources had revealed that on the afternoon of the Harveys' bottle-breaking altercation, at 13:30, Margot had noticed her husband's forgotten lunch. She had immediately driven to the veterinary clinic. Pulling up, Margot saw Dr. Harvey drive off, the girl in the passenger seat. Where were they heading? Would he want his sandwiches there?

A faux Tudor motor inn is a sad place to imagine a bright

young girl spending her last afternoon. As Terence approached the dilapidated structure, lumpy, stained mattresses were airing against the masonite walls; perhaps, the tiger thought, one of these had provided a screen upon which the girl could project her dreams . . . Sometimes, during detective work, the naive tiger found out things he would rather not have known. But the pure science of his profession, the jigsaw puzzle nature of crime, led him ever on.

Terence rolled his whiskers and waited. His bushland gang were a nimble crew. They could search small spaces; had a superior sense of smell; and most important, they knew this land, or an informant who did. With impeccable timing, Missy Pink-Princess sashayed from behind one of the box springs, purring. That scarlet kitty, that old painted pussycat's seen it all, thought Terence. Perfumed with the scent of musk and disinfectant, she had a husky meow he couldn't help but find arousing. She was big, a little rounder perhaps than she'd like to be, with huge green eyes.

Grrr! thought the tiger. She can make me extinct any damn way she likes!

Missy pointed her tail toward the room in which the couple had spent their last afternoon. Standing at the window, staring through the slit of open curtain, what gruesome sight did the distraught wife see? Once her eyes adjusted, what tangle of hot flesh, what writhing animal acts, did the beam of gritty light illuminate? Terence imagined Margot turning from the grimy motel window, destroyed, then driving home. He imagined her

*running inside her house, slamming shut the fly wire door, and
pouncing on the telephone. She needed help. She needed someone
to talk to, and so she dialed a help line.*

*Lifeline counselors are kindhearted volunteers wanting to
give something back to the community. But they often have lim-
ited life experience themselves, and can be completely ill equipped
to deal with emergencies. Following is the transcript of a conversation recorded the day before Margot Harvey disappeared:*

> *Lifeline:* What makes you sure he's being
>   unfaithful?
> *Margot:* I've just, I've just seen them . . .
> *Lifeline:* You've seen them together? In a motel
>   room? Speak up a little . . . Were they
>   copulating?
> *Margot* [almost inaudibly]: Yes.
> *Lifeline:* You're sure you're not just imagining
>   things?

*Terence, on reading this, sighed. He knew sexual jealousy could
produce pronounced physiological effects. In one university study
a group of married women was selected, and electrodes were
placed on the corrugater muscle in the brow, which contracted
when they frowned; skin conductance, or sweating, was also
tested, as was heart rate. The women were then shown doctored
footage of their spouses' infidelities. As the forged evidence became
more graphic their frowns increased by 7.09 units of contraction,*

the women sweated 4.02 microsiemens, and their heart rates accelerated by nearly ten beats per second, equivalent to drinking sixteen cups of coffee in one sitting. Terence read on, fearing the worst.

Lifeline: Well, this probably isn't the first time.

Margot: I beg your pardon?

Lifeline: He's probably had a finger in more than one pie for a while. The same thing happened to me. I was married for thirty years. I went away, for one week, to nurse my dying mother, and my husband started getting his end wet with a twenty-five-year-old waitress from down the street.

Margot: How dare she? How dare she?

Lifeline [sighing]: At first I was beside myself too, but life goes on. You've just got to get back on the horse . . . I find the work I do here, using my experiences to help other women, extremely gratifying . . . Are you there? . . . Hello? . . . Hello? Oh! She seems to have hung up.

TREMBLING, I WALKED further along a road I didn't know. Here, just 150 years ago, you could be sentenced to death for stealing a sheep. During public hangings the doomed man would stand on the gallows dressed in his convict's uniform, part gray, part canary yellow, the fool's costume on a pack of cards; and he would be jubilant, indeed triumphant, at having been granted an exit from this hell. It was hard to believe that my grandparents' grandparents were in the crowd watching the man laugh. My grandparents' generation certainly didn't speak of it: they were still touched by the stain. My parents' generation didn't speak of it because they had not been told. And at school my classmates and I didn't find this history the slightest bit related to us; even if it was, we didn't really care. Some of my friends at university got paid to welcome international visitors to the airport wearing convict costumes. We thought the joke was on the tourists.

With Lillian Hurnell's grudging approval I'd organized a field trip to Port Arthur for the fourth- and fifth-graders; some of the children's mothers, including Veronica, kindly volunteered to join us. *Murder at Black Swan Point* was newly released. She was a local celebrity, and I had no idea how much she knew.

The children and I were waiting for the bus when Mrs. Marne arrived, and we all stopped to look. She moved so smoothly, just an inch above the pavement. She seemed shy, her eyes averted to avoid some spotlight's glare. Gold bracelets rolled down her pale arms as she ran her fingers through her mane. "Lucien just adores you," she told me honey-voiced. "When I was little I prayed for a beautiful young teacher." She sat on one of the children's undersized benches, her long limbs collapsed by her side. It was as if she was dozy with her own charisma; she'd ingested it in pill form, finding it too strong. Lucien stood next to her protectively, while the other children played chasey around them.

The kids had dressed for the day in ripped jeans and stained T-shirts. There were a few pickpockets; a few forgers; and a number who claimed to have been sent down for food-related crimes. The gourmands sympathized with hungry Thomas Chaddick, who "did pluck up, spoil and destroy" twelve cucumbers. The coquettes had committed crimes similar to James Grace, an eleven-year-old who'd stolen ten yards of ribbon and a pair of silk stockings. Danielle had brought to school talcum powder and a mascara wand; so a subset of the female convicts was pale and beauty-spotted, although there was no mention of underage harlots. Girls were really only bit players in local convict history. Women were sent down to Van Diemen's Land because "unnatural crimes" were rife amongst the male convicts. They were then locked up, miles from the men, in a separate Hobart penitentiary called The Female Factory. There was now a fudge factory on this site. Inside the old sandstone walls, truffles were handmade.

When the bus arrived, Veronica rose, stretching to her full thin height. As though for the children's benefit, she and I traded excited smiles. Veronica was wearing a beige linen pantsuit. It gave the impression she was going on a high-class safari, except that her shoes were as delicate as ballet slippers. All the other mothers, and I, wore sneakers and flannel shirts like campers. But there'd been no real need for us to dress down; we weren't going traipsing through the bush and I wished I'd made an effort too. Veronica and another mother sat at the front of the bus, chatting at low volume. I strained to hear what they were saying, but was partnered with Henry Ledder, who'd been misbehaving. Henry had his front teeth blacked, and claimed to have stolen two spoons like his great-great-great-grandfather. We'd been driving for a while before I turned to him: "What's the worst thing a person can do?"

"The worst thing?" Henry mused. "To go to jail after shooting someone." He didn't quite know how to differentiate the crime from the punishment. This was referred to as the preconventional stage of moral development, typifying the moral world of children under nine, and many adult criminal offenders.

"What's the worst thing that happens to children?" I asked, immediately realizing the question's impropriety.

"Dominic's mother was looking out the window, and she saw a little kid being chopped up," Henry told me wide-eyed, "all into little pieces, just down on the street."

"What did Dominic's mother do?"

"She screamed."

"Henry, that's not true!"

"They saw it. Well maybe they didn't see it happen, but they saw the remains."

He actually said *remains*. Attempting to change the subject, I asked, "What's the worst thing that happens to kids on TV?"

"A bad boy turns into a dog," Henry advised quickly, as if reciting multiplication tables.

"Oh!" I poked him lightly, trying to recast this chat as something jolly. "Dominic's mother never saw that. And you'll transform into a dog yourself if you tell such silly stories!" Henry looked confused. Children's sense of the political world was usually fairly abstract. In an American study it was found candy store attendants were considered to be government employees by at least 70 percent of kindergarten students; a policeman, after the president, was believed to hold the most power.

We pulled up at Port Arthur. The remains of the penal settlement looked ancient, but each ruined monument was still Georgian in ideal. Convict-made bricks, the colors of the cliffs, rose to form a neat village of half-buildings. The church's steeple was long gone and birds darted through the bell tower. In the penitentiary, yellow daisies and milk-thistle carpeted the cells' floors. None of the buildings had a ceiling, just high brick walls, with crude windows framing the most uncanny views: serene Opossum Bay; rolling green hills; an English country garden of weeping willows, hollyhocks, and snapdragon, planted by the homesick officers. The remnants of this gentrified Port Arthur could stun you. It was like stumbling upon an Arcadia with only the whipbird, its long high cry and sudden note change, reminding you of the horror that existed here.

After the complex was closed down in the 1870s, the local community hoped to transform Port Arthur into a health resort, "the Brighton of the Australias," but the damp weather proved off-putting. Instead two pianos were put in the penitentiary's dining hall, and some nights people danced until day broke. Young couples arrived with picnics and all the ladies squealed as their beaux pretended to lock them in the cells. Day-trippers visited by the hundred, and this tourism funded jetties and new roads. Then bushfires swept through, and the settlement burned to the ground. When, in *The Scarlet Letter,* Nathaniel Hawthorne describes prisons as "the black flowers of civilization," he could have been describing the charred remains of the convict boys' cabinet-making, their hand-carved church pews turned to cinders.

Inside the cultural center was a re-creation of a convict ship's hulk. A tape played creaking bottom-of-the-boat sounds, with ominous cockney mutterings thrown in for full effect. A display board, nailed to the ship's wall, used visual props to contrast the convicts' crimes with their punishments. *Life for stealing a flute:* an educator had attached some CDs with a glue gun. *Seven years for stealing tobacco:* a carton of cigarettes had been stuck on; but by now, all were pilfered. *Life for stealing a watch:* there was the glue outline of a watch from before it was ripped down. "This is all very progressive," Veronica observed, sidling up to me. She had a face drawn in light. "We learned nothing at all, nothing." Reaching over she brushed something out of my hair. "A little bit of twig . . . now all gone." She smiled a pursed-lipped smile, her chin crinkling.

The Endport Primary classes were split into smaller groups. Veronica finessed that she and I would be in one group, and we were led away, accompanied by ten children. Our guide, Malcolm, was about my age, tall and thin, with dark shoulder-length hair kept untidy to disguise a baby face. He wore a three-piece suit and a high white collar like an old-fashioned undertaker. He seemed to lead from his knees, his legs long streaks of black. Two by two, the children—carrying their worksheets—followed him out amongst the ruins. Veronica and I, walking next to each other, trailed behind.

"Malcolm's cute," Veronica whispered. "If I were young and single, I'd pounce."

I laughed.

"Do you have a boyfriend?"

"No," I replied, a little defensively. "Not really."

"Well, there's hardly rich pickings in Endport," she whispered. "Get his number!"

I laughed again, nervously: even if I hadn't been having an affair with her husband, this sort of conversation would have made me uncomfortable. It was not as though historically I'd had a lot of success with men my own age. I didn't always find them easy to talk to. I guessed they were just immature. Plus, they seemed to find me really intense and weird. Like the Eleanor Siddell of my imagination, I went to an all-girls' school from age four to eighteen. I kissed a boy for the first time at a party when I was seventeen and unfortunately it turned out he was a kleptomaniac. Apparently he'd steal other boys' books, then stand in the queue at the school's secondhand bookshop, whiting out the owners' names with correction fluid. One day the fluid didn't dry in time, and he was suspended. I didn't know about this until I came to school on the Monday morning after the party, and all the girls lined up asking me if I'd happened to see their gold earrings, or their mother's purse: items, they claimed, he'd probably stolen. Sometimes I'd see that boy around, but I never spoke to him again. Later people said he had gone to jail.

Malcolm took us inside the museum, a building originally built for the insane—he explained that a lot of convicts went insane after being left too long in the dumb-cells, a form of solitary confinement without any light. On display was a secret society of forgotten objects: a yellowing collection of pressed seaweed once belonging to the minister's wife; the remains of some convicts' shoes; a whalebone walking stick; an emu leg. Malcolm led the children to a wall showing off a range of torturers' equipment: leg irons; a vast selection of balls and chains; muskets and pistols.

The convict ship *Isabella*, he told us, arrived in 1834 with the first load of boy convicts bound for the children's prison opposite Port Arthur—Point Puer. The boys had all arrived drunk, having broken into a store of wine in the ship's hold meant for the officers. Once they'd sobered up they were trained as bakers, carpenters, sawyers, tailors, shoemakers. "They were schooled very slightly, encouraged to repent, and punished." Malcolm pointed to a cat-o'-nine-tails. "This whip would be soaked in brine to make the leather tougher." He spoke softly in a lilt, the way people do in Irish folksongs. He had told his stories many times before and now he paused with slightly manufactured woe, or rushed through dreadful details as though no longer interested. A silver ring of Celtic design, on his middle finger, flashed as he gestured; "Two lashes took the skin off to the bone, but transgressors could be sentenced to up to three hundred lashes. All the skin on a man's back would be flying in the breeze." Malcolm's eyes were bright. "He would go to the infirmary with the scarlet scars of the cat. They'd take a bandage off someone else, dunk it in cold water, then reuse it on him."

"Malcolm's nervous," Veronica told me. "I think he likes you."

"*Nooo*," I said blushing.

She giggled. "*Ye-es.*"

"Well, it's great he's not mollycoddling the kids," I conceded. "He's talking to them like to short adults." I sighed. In art the day before, the children had each made a "silver tray" by gluing string onto a piece of cardboard, and covering it with aluminum foil. The art teacher had gotten this idea from an American book on pioneers—you could also make a rag rug or homemade cough drops. I thought this sent out mixed messages. The convict children learned trades, but not silversmithing. And how many Tasmanian pioneers had the gentility to make themselves cough drops? It was enough just to be consumptive; they didn't need to accessorize.

Malcolm explained to us that at Point Puer there was Sir George's set of rules, obviously, but there were also the boys' shadow rules. A terrifying natural order emerged. Malcolm turned on a torch, despite the now plentiful sunlight, and shone it in the children's faces. "There was a black economy, and the boys would try to steal from the colonial officials' houses to gain advantage. John Pollard!"—he pointed the torch at Alastair—"was charged with being *absent from Divine Service without authority, the Catechist's house having been broken into.* William Bowles!"—he targeted Henry—"was charged with *having buttons improperly in his possession and being suspected of gambling.* William Cummins! He must have benefited from an illicit exchange, only to spend four days in solitary confinement on bread and water for *having a pipe and tobacco in his possession improperly and smoking near the Superintendent's Quarters.*" Malcolm's voice grew low with suspense. "As Sir George's system became underfunded and overfull, even the pettiest misdemeanor invited punishment." He paused. "The boys lied to anyone in any position of authority, they sang hymns like banshees. At night, they would turn out the lights and attack their convict watchmen, pouring the contents of the chamber pots over their heads. In one scuffle, a guard was hospitalized for three months." Malcolm shone the torch under his own chin. "Another time, a man died."

Pleased by this, the children strolled around filling in their worksheets. Veronica stood looking in the display cases, tilting her head different ways as if each sorry item needed to be considered from all perspectives. I followed her example: what struck me as the museum's strangest exhibit was a re-creation of what a cell for the insane would have been like. There was a door and you bent down and opened a little flap to see a wax dummy, dressed up as a convict, standing—there was only room to stand—wearing a ball and chain. "Convicts were only taken out of the dumb-cells, in hoods, to go to church."

I turned. Malcolm was standing behind me. I blushed as he pointed to a leather mask. "Flies crawled over their faces.

Officers stood up the front of the chapel making sure the convicts' lips moved only in prayer."

I bent to look again, flattered by this attention. Now people had started throwing coins into the mock cell. The whole of the floor was covered with twenty-cent pieces. "Do you think they were thrown in out of sympathy?" I asked. "Or to make a wish?" There was something awful about the silver lying there, shining its promise before a mannequin, which stood in for someone who had been mute.

Malcolm cleared his throat. "It's money standing in for shit."

I looked at him surprised, but thought of one of the children's running conversations.

> Lucien: *My dad believes, and I think it's a very sensible idea, that not God, but a being that is bigger than God, created us for his amusement. Umm, that guy might invite one of his friends around just for a brief play with us, and one of their days could be like several million years for us.*
> Eliza: *The world began when God made a big bang!*
> Lucien: *How could a bang do anything? I think of a giant holding an ant farm and he's looking down; any second that giant could go, "Ah no, that's a big no-no." Pqueew! "Bye-bye!" And then it's suddenly like your back's broken in two by some unknown force.*
> Eliza: *We can believe what we want!*
> Lucien: *A bang would do nothing!*
> Billy: *Wait! I think they should see how many countries believe in God and have an election.*

We broke for lunch and I ushered the kids outside. Veronica strolled next to her son, but neither of them spoke. For Lucien there was clearly a mix of pleasure and humiliation in having his beautiful mother present. He was proud of her, but it was embarrassing the other children should see her trying to feed *him*—the class gothic—a salmon and avocado sandwich. It was also embarrassing that she should witness his lack of popularity. I had begun to suspect the class mailbox had evolved into nothing more than a mechanism for spreading malice toward him. The little girls opened up notes and dissolved into mean giggles; the same giggles as when he walked through the door each morning. They all had crushes on him. He was Byronic; at nine years, with his curled lip and knowledge of Hell, he appreciated the tropes of the greatest romantics, and even *I* wanted to meet up with him again, when he was twenty-one, to talk about the cosmos.

I had imagined Lucien's parents were very supportive of his intellectual precocity, although Lucien gave the impression things at home were fiery. The children often complained about their parents—"They don't know what fun is." "They think you're silly." "They don't understand what you like to eat"—but one time Lucien had been quite upset. He wouldn't venture into the playground all lunchtime, and, after skirting around the question, I finally asked, "Is everything okay with Mum and Dad?" "Well," he said softly, "they don't really understand how it feels. You can be having a friendly dispute, because there's no relationship without a few bumps in it, and they'll say, 'That's it! Go to your room! No pocket money for a year! No TV!' And it was just a little dispute." He shook his head, looking sad. "I don't understand how they can go ballistic when they've been perfectly calm for the last half hour." "Kids do that too," I'd rallied. Lucien had sighed. "We naturally have short fuses," he'd explained, "but they should have longer ones. They've been alive a lot longer, and they've taken more insults and stuff."

Veronica gave her son a moist-wipe, encouraging him to clean his face. Lucien took it and dabbed himself without conviction. He didn't know whether to sit with Veronica or to play with the other kids. A group of boys were hobbling around the picnic tables trying to pick each other's pockets. Then, without even being locked up, they time-traveled to the point at which they were breaking out of jail. They'd heard escapees survived on whale blubber scraped off the rocks; seaweed; wallaby; the odd black swan's rancid carcass. The children all reeled around, delighting in their nausea. The convicts might not have known how to swim, but they did. They mimed freestyle around the lawn with only Darren stopping to force Alastair's drowning. In their faux rags they looked like a children's theater troupe performing the off-cuts of *Oliver!* Lucien ran into the fray and the kids stopped to renegotiate. They had heard of one convict who, trying to escape overland, found a dead kangaroo and wrapped himself in the animal's fur. Lucien was allowed to be the kangaroo man, and Darren and Henry were suddenly the officers out hunting the ingredient for kangaroo tail soup.

"Boys!" I called out in warning. They ignored me.

> Miss Byrne: *What is a law?*
> Alastair: *A law says kids can't drink beer.*
> Miss Byrne: *What would happen if there were no laws?*

Eliza: *People would steal a lot more and cars would run
into each other and there would be murder all over
the place and we would have an awful, cruel, fighting
country.*

"Boys!" Behind them rose the half-buildings, made amber by
the sun. The penitentiary looked like a child's unfinished
sketch of a house with many windows. It was hardly as if living in a civil society was natural to us, I thought, annoyed.
We obviously didn't have to go back many generations to
find a state of utter lawlessness, coexisting alongside the Dra-
conian. In the museum, while Veronica had been admiring
herself in the reflective glass, I'd read of one of Australia's first
contributions to the true-crime genre. It was the diary of the
escaped convict turned bushranger Michael Howe. In 1818,
Howe's knapsack was found containing a book he'd made
from kangaroo skin. Inside, with the blood of the animals
he'd slaughtered, he'd written down his dreams. He'd written
of his victims seeking retribution. He'd written of the other
bushrangers he'd betrayed, and of Aborigines killing him.
He'd written of his sister, whom he loved, back in England.
And of wanting to live in a nice house with a little garden. In
blood, he'd listed the fruit, flowers, and vegetables he hoped
one day to grow.

I watched the boys playing, and it occurred to me you
could do a fabulous re-creation of Howe's diary for young
readers. Children would love the kangaroo-fur cover and
scarlet print. The story had the gore; it had the mystery; it
had the pathos. It was so subtle you could *only* read between
the lines to understand that in Chapter One boatloads of

British riffraff spilled out. Runaway convicts, like the blood diarist himself, learned bushcraft from the Aborigines and disappeared into the bush. Meanwhile the Aborigines, terrified of the colonists' guns *vomiting forth thunder*, had their land cleared. Dispossessed, they formed raiding parties, lighting decoy fires to steal settlers' guns and food. Settlers were speared, but during the seven-year Black War the whites that died did not surpass the number that arrived monthly on each new convict ship. And by 1839 most of the indigenous population had died or been driven away. Our local history is the *Ur*-true-crime story, and in volume after volume the bodies pile up. The government placed a bounty on Michael Howe, and the bushranger was discovered living like a wildman, wearing kangaroo skins in a tiny hut covered with flowers. His killers decapitated him and his head was placed on display in Hobart.

"Henry and Darren!" I yelled. "Stop that immediately!"

I turned. Veronica was watching me. She became sleepy again, stretching. She touched at a thin string of seed pearls around her neck like at a rosary. I cleared my throat. The pearls looked like puffed rice. "It must be incredibly hard in your profession," I said, "having to concentrate day in, day out on such brutality."

"Incredibly," she answered lightly. "It was incredibly hard. I was so squeamish; even terrified of blood when I started. But still, like everyone else, I'd rather read about a crime of passion." Veronica smiled. "Of course, they're the most romantic crimes; the ones we respond to most vehemently. Who gets worked up about white-collar crime? Who really cares about money laundering or embezzling?"

"No one does."

"Exactly." We both laughed, and this laughter made us intimate. We turned to watch the children as they continued escaping. "Lucien does think you're lovely," Veronica said again. "When I was little we always had such sadists as teachers." She touched my arm, adding, "You really got the feeling they despised children; all soaking their whips in brine."

"You've got to love children in this profession," I told her quickly, "just to do the job."

Veronica raised an eyebrow. "I can imagine."

"And your son is such a terrific smart kid."

"Thank you."

Lucien was tearing Darren from a shark's jaws, then whittling a spear. I chuckled, expecting Veronica to join me. She smiled slightly sadly; " I don't think he's got any of my genes at all. In photos of him and his father around the same age, it's uncanny." She shook her head. "You can't pick them apart." For a moment she looked wistful, then she turned to me, holding out a sandwich. "Lucien won't eat this. Would you like it?"

"Oh, thank you."

At that moment, I wanted more than anything for Veronica to like me. I had no problem suspending belief that I was her husband's lover. In fact, perhaps I never had been: I was her friend. Being able to say, "Yes, Veronica is a great woman" seemed very mature. It struck me there was something so pure about her. I guessed that was the irony. You probably needed that purity to embark on such a brave, gory project—if you were already exhausted and cynical, it would all be too much. I took another bite, savoring the salmon. Since Veronica had brought it to my attention, I now thought perhaps Malcolm was catching my eye and giving me meaningful glances. While we ate lunch he stood staring out at the bay. He'd skip a pebble, then look back to make sure we were watching. It was impressive that he felt so passionately about all this history. Only just obscured, over the water, were the Suicide Cliffs which marked the eastern side of Point Puer. I saw Malcolm skip another pebble. "Oh, this sandwich is good!"

"Lucien even runs like his father."

I held the bread, staring at the water.

"He runs and his arms barely move."

"Really?"

She gestured over the bay, shaking her head. "My husband finds my connection to the Black Swan Point crime slightly . . . repellent," Veronica confided. "He's very old-fashioned. But while writing the book I walked with him around the cliffs and I had to acknowledge there's a struggle within all of us . . . An eye for an eye."

I didn't speak.

"You know, Kate, you get to an age and your whole body starts to fall apart," Veronica said. "A lot of the women I know are having their eyes done. My best friend just fixed her breasts." She saw my expression and added, "I understand it—she's thinking of getting a divorce—and I've felt them." Veronica laughed briefly. "Lou told me about it while we were shopping. Very funny, us in a changing room; she lifting up her shirt for me to have a squeeze." She paused. "They weren't rocklike. Listen, all I'm saying is I understand it, but I'm not doing it. If I did it I'd still look like a forty-year-old woman. Why try to look like a *neat* forty-year-old woman?"

I wasn't sure what to say. "Well . . . the thing is, for every wrinkle there's more wisdom."

"No, there's just another wrinkle." Her voice grew businesslike; she was finally waking. "My friend found out the hard way that men reach a certain age, and they want to fuck around, because they only can for about five more minutes, and they want young flesh. 'So, fine,' I say to her. 'Let them fuck.' You know? You don't have to take a knife to yourself."

"You can take a knife," I began, before I could stop myself, "to the young flesh."

She laughed. "That's good, that's quite good."

After lunch, Malcolm stared out to where the convict ships would have dropped anchor. The children followed his gaze, disappointment clouding their faces. There was now a luxury cruise ship parked in Opossum Bay, but what had they expected? A chain of skulls strung together? Pickpockets' loot hidden under loose rock? I could hear my heart beating.

Malcolm pointed toward a small island, covered with eucalyptus, in the middle of the bay: "In between Port Arthur and Point Puer is *L'Isle des Morts*," he announced dramatically, before admitting the convicts referred to their burial site as Dead Island. "The officers had headstones facing toward England; the convicts' mass graves faced in the opposite direction. The gravedigger was a giant man who walked with a cane in each hand," he continued. "The authorities were relieved when he volunteered to live by himself on the island, because he had a diabolical temper and often broke the other convicts' legs with one swipe of a cane." Malcolm paused for the cartoon to register. "Gravedigging was a permanent position: partly because he couldn't swim, and everyone thought the bay was so infested you could walk to Dead Island, and back, on the heads of sharks." He paused again—half historian, half stand-up comedian. "The gravedigger stayed on the island, having dug his own grave in the nicest spot, until he began to be haunted." The children all laughed. "He had to light a bonfire so someone would row over to save him."

Malcolm started to recite a convict ballad that no one, now, knew the music to.

> *Isle of the dead! well might*
> *Thy verdant bosom be,*
> *The last retreat of honor fair*
> *The death home of the free*
> *But moldering there, the slave of crime*
> *And wretch of blighted name*
> *Sink in the dread repose of guilt*
> *To rest in graves of shame.*

I breathed deeply, trying to remain calm. Malcolm, with his medallion profile, definitely invested a lot of emotion in all this. The children stood listening to his powerful voice, a crew of Artful Dodgers arrested by boredom. I wished they would pay more attention. It wouldn't be long until no one in our culture could be bothered to memorize these ballads. And it was not as though the children were thinking of their country's history. Of course they weren't. They were thinking: "Those bus seats smelled of banana peel and sweat." The bus seats had smelled bad—they'd been upholstered in a thick synthetic material with a colorful pattern which brought to mind vomiting tropical fish. The children were hoping: "Please don't make me sit next to Darren on the bus ride back." Darren had made Alastair count roadkill all along the highway: "That was an old sock!" "No, it was a squashed cat, I swear!" An older teacher once confided that when he heard of children being badly beaten, he now thought, Yeah, and what had the kid done? I listened to the ballad, wondering if there were any reliable statistics as to how many of my students were descended from degenerates transported in the nineteenth century.

Isle of the homeless dead!
Within thy rock-bound breast,
Full many a heart that throbb'd for home
Now find untroubl'd rest;
For home, alas! they throbb'd in vain;
A mother's fond caress,
A father's care, a sister's smile,
Has ceas'd their hearts to bless.

After a few more verses, I found myself thinking of the Marnes sleeping together. My face flushed. Early on, Thomas had gripped me by the arm, demanding, "So, what have you done?" I hadn't known what he was talking about. "Have you ever slept with a woman?" he'd asked hopefully. "No." He tried again: "Have you ever slept with two men?" "No," I'd answered, "have you?" He shook his head. "Have you ever slept with three men?" I'd asked. "Four?"

Had Veronica done these things? How many perversions could she check off?

More recently Thomas had told me about a case he'd come across, a Tasmanian bestiality trial: a husband had come home, found his wife with their rottweiler, and had shot the dog. Apparently the husband had filmed various videos of this happening before, so he shouldn't have been completely surprised. And perhaps as a result, the wife had decided to sue him. "She could be suing him for infringement of property," Thomas had explained, his face calm, handsome. "If someone shoots your dog it's trespass on your dog. The cost of replacing the animal she could certainly recover, provided it was *her* dog." He made a steeple with his fingers on which to rest his chin. "But unless this was a 'working dog,' as it were, a breeding dog, it would be difficult to recover further damages." For a moment he was silent. "This is how I'd handle the case: it strikes me that if the woman was in a loving relationship with the dog, and her old man came home and shot the dog, she could bring an action against the husband for negligence resulting in nervous shock." "What's nervous shock?" I'd asked. "Well, one of the symptoms is loss of sexual function." Later, I'd wondered what he'd really been trying to tell me.

Initially with Thomas I had been willfully innocent. It was convenient to play the obstinate naïf rather than confront the consequences of his sexual urbanity. "Was this the way people really behaved?" I would ask myself in mock affront. "Not the woman and the man, nor their dog. I mean the people who told these stories—Thomas and Veronica at their kitchen table, so worldly they don't give two hoots in hell about an abused puppy!" Then I'd shake my head, like any normal person, at how bizarre, at how terrifying, people managed to make sex.

On and on the thing went: *isle of the exil'd dead! isle of the fetter'd dead! isle of the unwep't dead!* After the ballad's ninth verse, Veronica leaned toward me. "I've decided that I hate Malcolm," she whispered. I turned to her. "Sociopath," she mouthed, as he continued reciting this tedious convict ballad no one even had the music to. I studied him more closely. "You're right," I whispered back. Perhaps, after all was said and done, younger men were a waste of time. Yes, he was cute. But didn't people with weird proclivities get attracted to these dark, sadistically charged places? Then again, if I felt some deviant vibe off him, was I just recognizing a part of myself? Veronica's book had neglected to acknowledge that these horrific crimes were not just the things other people did. These deeds were with us; they were in our nervous systems. We read true-crime books to learn about ourselves.

Danielle: *In a perfect world things would get all crowded because there wouldn't be killers to kill people. And no one would get sick, and it would get all crowded.*

Henry: *But just say there were killers, and say there's reincarnation—well, you'd choose which animal you'd reincarnate into, you'd just go, "A lion!" and kill the person who killed you.*

Anaminka: *I think in a perfect world maybe we'd be something else, other than a person. Scientists say we've been fish before, and they say we've had gills before.*

Billy: *That's something you can't prove. Like you can't prove if we were, but you can't prove that we're not.*

The ballad finished and I nudged Anaminka. She stared at the ground, blushing, as she thanked Malcolm on behalf of Endport Primary. I looked over the water, with rising anxiety. It was small consolation realizing Veronica knew so much about rage and humiliation because she was married to a chronic adulterer. No wonder she'd chosen to write *Murder at Black Swan Point.* No wonder there'd been such satisfaction in making all a life's tributaries flow irresistibly toward doom. Do you think Margot enjoyed the murder? I asked myself. Do you think she enjoyed cutting the girl up? Of course she did. You have to take your pleasure where you find it.

We headed back to the cultural center, Veronica walking next to her son. I'd realized that I understood her book much better when I gave Margot her face. When I thought of the things I did with Thomas, it was no leap at all to imagine her beautiful reserve and cool asides hiding someone out of control. But of course there was another intimacy for which Margot must have hated Ellie.

I watched Veronica looking over Lucien's worksheet. Margot must have hated Ellie for touching her children: for putting her face next to the little girls' faces; for stroking the girls' soft hair. Ellie probably touched Margot's children tenderly, engineering it so that if the girls' daddy walked into the reception room he'd see the kids draped all over his lover, fawning all over her; and he'd smile, so proud of this happy little family. Margot probably walked into the clinic and she had to fight with her daughters just to put their shoes on. She had to fight with them just to put their socks on, and the sock had to be lined up perfectly on the little foot. Then her daughter would pull her foot away, readjusting the sock so many times that Margot wanted to snap her ankle, and shove the foot into the shoe. And Ellie—"that bitch," Margot thought—watched all of this like she was the good mummy. And Margot would drive home barely able to breathe, thinking of how she'd teach that girl a lesson.

I was exhausted: the children were so completely alive in this dead place. They waltzed and wrestled while behind them the building's facades looked diseased. These buildings had seen the end of the world and would keep rotting until they were just piles of bricks. This was Sir George's mill to grind criminals into God-fearing citizens. His failed Utopia. And in our discussions the children and I had surely hit upon Sir George's impasse: "Why in his omnipotence and benevolence does God allow evil to occur?" If God could make the perfect world why did this place even exist?

> Billy: *The world would probably be something like eighty-five percent good. It's just the murderers and robbers and all that. If they were off it, I reckon this world would be a perfect world.*
>
> Danielle: *In a perfect world you wouldn't need to go to school or have libraries because you'd know all that. And you could do all that. And you would be perfect and you could do anything. You could fly.*

Veronica linked arms with me. "I want us to hang out. Perhaps when my husband can baby-sit we could run away for an evening, and have a little drink." She tore a page out of her diary and wrote down her phone number. "Just call anytime if you're lonely, or want a chat, or feel scared all alone there." She smiled at me conspiratorially. "It's been great getting acquainted." She shook her head. "I think you're wonderful."

Turning, she looked back to where the divers had searched for Margot. Veronica leaned in close, confiding they'd had little success. "The water was so full of silt and seaweed that the divers couldn't see a thing. They swam in semicircles, the palms of their hands searching the sea floor for a body. The men could only be lowered down twice a day, for fifteen minutes, when the tides were the least dangerous, so fierce are these currents."

I stared across flat, gray Opossum Bay. Veronica added softly, "Around the eastern side, the waters are full of sharks and sea lice. Bodies disappear there constantly." I felt myself starting to spin. She sighed: "Still, the divers claimed if Margot had been down there, they would've probably found some trace . . ."

I had to excuse myself.

People speculated that Mrs. Harvey could have been alive. After all, she was well connected, she had access to a fair amount of money. Maybe, like Veronica's "friend," she'd had plastic surgery and had come back to work at the bakery so as to be able to see her daughters. She gave them extra jam tarts whenever they placed an order. Maybe she took a job as their cleaner. She still cleaned their toilet, but she had the satisfaction of having destroyed Graeme's life the way he had tried to destroy hers. She was selling apples on a chair by the side of a road. She was wearing a parachute-silk tracksuit, walking in slow motion down the main street . . . Or she was a sylph, in a low-slung silver sports car, cruising around harassing the wanton. She'd married again and had, say, one child—a boy—and maybe she'd even done something to bring attention to her previous persona's plight. She'd *written a book*.

When the school bus arrived, my name had to be called out over the center's loudspeaker. I was in the women's toilets on my hands and knees, retching until I'd lost the sandwich.

FINALLY I CAME upon an inlet where the foundations of an old jetty rose like driftwood soldiers marching over undulating mud. A rotted-out rowboat lay nearby. Someone, rowing along, had suddenly realized the flood was over and silence had then calcified everything left. I'd been stumbling along this dirt road, praying for some sign of life. Now, opposite the jetty, shone the windows of a small weather-board house. The house was painted sage, long yellowed by the sun. A utility truck with oversized headlights was parked in the drive, its front wheel chained to a nearby tree. The surrounding garden seemed full of detritus picked off the mudflats. Plastic buckets, lost from their toy spades, were planted with geraniums. Flower beds, lined with shells, hosted arrangements of petrified wood, a collection of broken paddles, the skull of a large bird. Then strangely, in the middle of this sea junk, appeared a white fountain tiered like a wedding cake.

The effect, overall, wasn't necessarily welcoming. Somebody had written warnings on the plastic lids of ice-cream containers before nailing them to trees. *No bike riding*—in awkward, strangled letters—*No trespassing. Beware of Dog.* There was a fence made of driftwood; and behind it, a small dog barked strangely. "Hello!" I shouted in the direction of the house. "Hello!"

Nothing happened. Taking the apple out of my pocket, and ignoring the handwritten signs, I opened the gate. The dog ran toward me, squealing. Holding the apple away from my body, I tried to encourage it to keep its distance. I didn't want it to touch me and I did a kind of two-step every time it approached. The dog had no tail and a shiny black coat, pointy little teeth and the fine legs of a pig. If you avoided its line of vision it became confused, forgetting about you. It snuffled around in the dirt, its hoggy arse in the air, and one felt sure this creature must have sprung from the loins of a pig. Then it looked up, all dog, and chased its phantom tail in retarded little circles. The animal started sniffing around my ankles. It leaped, leaning its front paws against my calf. I took a bite out of the apple, spitting the chunk on the ground. I jerked my leg: the hog-dog deferred to the apple.

"You have a problem?" a deep voice asked.

I spun around to face the dog's owner: a very large, mustached man. He was in his early forties with swollen, gray-blue eyes. Under each lid, dark rings were carved into his face so deeply it seemed he'd forgotten how to sleep. "Your dog certainly likes apple," I said, glancing down. The man continued staring at me. "Oh, I'm sorry, I'm Kate Byrne, I was driving nearby, and . . ." I felt nauseous. "There was a problem with my brakes." I looked up at his house. A woman was standing by the door, an incredibly thin woman with long hair. "I was wondering if I could use your phone." I forced a smile. "Or, if you could make a call for me . . . to a nearby garage."

"There is no nearby garage."

"The car started whistling, this awful whistling, and then I was pumping the brakes, but . . ."

"How far off?"

"I've been walking for an hour."

"So, you'll probably also be wanting a ride back?"

He opened the gate. I paused and waved at the thin woman; she saw me and went back inside. A moment later their fountain sprayed on, but she did not return. "What's your dog's name?" I asked, breaking the silence. It wasn't the kind of animal you'd just call Rover.

"Bullet."

"That's a good name."

He led me toward the house, then paused. On a windowsill were rows of plastic dolls; they wore ballooning crocheted skirts, the kind people use as tea cozies or toilet paper covers. He thought better of taking me inside, and I followed him behind the house to a corrugated iron shed. The shed was concrete-floored and cold, stinking of something metallic. Each of his tools had been outlined in black on the fibrowall. But it seemed he was lax putting them back in place: silhouettes showed two handsaws on the loose, a wrench and large screwdriver also unaccounted for. I had no idea what the man would make here. Outside old farm equipment and pieces of scrap metal were lying around.

"I'll go and get ready," he told me.

"Well." I smiled. "I'll be here."

He left and I walked in tiny circles of panic. The back wall was made of fly wire, and although I could see no flies, I could hear their high-pitched howl. Part of the concrete was carpeted with kangaroo skins, but I didn't like to stand on them. A boy I knew once told me, "When you shoot your first kangaroo you expect the world to change, bells to ring, but nothing happens." Walking over a rug I kicked up the corner and stamped the skin back in place, feeling stupidly apologetic. The man's workbench ran along one wall. I inspected it from end to end, then looked up and saw a picture ripped from a magazine of a woman with her legs spread wide. "Please God, help me."

Inside the house, the man and the woman started fighting. She raised her voice. It was shrill, furious. There'd be a break, then she'd start again. I'd obviously interrupted them in the middle of some dispute. A tiny piece of oxidized mirror hung on the shed's wall: I stood in snagged panty hose and high heels, my clothes crushed and dirty from jumping out of the car. I had dressed for the hotel, but now just looked whorish. I couldn't hear exactly what the woman was screaming, although I began to feel perhaps it involved me. Why would she want to help? Why would she want *him* to help? Her voice rose again, then suddenly stopped. I continued waiting.

This space: it smelled of man. It smelled of men when they were alone. I wished suddenly that my father, or my grandfather, had better prepared me for how foreign men were. I wondered what they even thought, with those blank faces. It was like gauging the sea. In high school we sat in sex education and blew up condoms, sending them flying across the room, but no one mentioned that when men made polite conversation it would always seem like an interaction that had been dubbed.

I stared at the ripped picture. There was no sound now in

the house, which was slightly worse. I squatted next to a tap to wash my face and hands. Outside, it was beginning to grow dark. I brushed dirt off my skirt, realizing my problem wasn't even the clothes I was wearing. It was my body, unfortunately feminine, underneath. I would never get over the shock of developing breasts: the injustice of having no say in your own body's design. As I waited for the man to come back, I counted all the reasons I had to hate Thomas.

When I'd first told him about the class philosophy sessions he'd suggested that I teach the children about Nietzsche. I'd rejected the idea after checking in the *World Book Encyclopedia*—"There was no perfect world, no truth, no God." "People should live their lives like works of art." "Plato was to blame for everything." I now groaned. Thomas didn't really believe any of that. His bleak theories were only used to put out libidinous spot fires. All his amorality depended on his being married. When I raised with Thomas the late-night phone calls, he wore a smug look as if imagining Veronica and me mud-wrestling. If I pushed the point, he became quietly furious. The theme of his sulking: do you really think this possible of my refined wife? His adulterous side was just his dreaming. And I was a character in the dream. I could shriek on and on about Veronica's disturbed nature, but he would drive back to his very straight life, laughing at my rants as one laughs at any crazy who abuses you in your sleep. Would it come too late, the moment in which he woke up? Later, Graeme Harvey would have remembered his own state of oblivion. "Of course this was going to happen!" he would have cried. "Of course!" one always cries, rolled by the shadow of *what if?*

The man came back into the shed wearing a guerrilla print suit. He was holding a glass of raspberry cordial. "I thought you might be thirsty," he said. Quickly I moved away from the spreadeagled legs and took the glass, thanking him. I shouldn't drink this, I thought, raising it to my lips. The sugary liquid ran down my throat: I imagined the paralysis starting from my feet, then working up. The man was big, powerful, but his slumped shoulders gave a lurching quality to his movements as if his arms were far too long. He collected a stretch of rope, then a plastic tarpaulin. I was frightened of offending him, but I couldn't drink all the cordial. He'd mixed it too sweet.

The man led me again past the row of dolls. The woman was nowhere in sight. He led me through the strange garden and started unchaining the truck's front wheel from the tree. He fixed a rope to a cage-like structure, made from old clothing racks, that had been welded to the truck's chassis. Bullet sniffed at my ankles. I thought of a dog and a pig together; a pig baby swelling in the dog. Bullet squealed, leaning its paws on my calf. The panty hose tore further. I wondered if this man had let the pig impregnate the dog for sport. Then, as if reading my mind, he turned, grabbing the evidence—this yelping creature—by the collar, tossing it aside. I cleared my throat. "You've got a great view here." He looked out at the abandoned jetty, at all the mud, but said nothing.

We got into the truck and drove away. Behind my head was a gun rack where two rifles were resting. "Thank you so much for doing this," I murmured. "I really appreciate it." All the tools missing from his shed wall rolled around on the floor under the passenger seat. I tried to hold my skirt down, level with my knees. Evening was falling; twilight to keep you punch-drunk. We drove slowly into all the little minutes where nothing happens. There was nothing to fill you up here but the casuarinas making their *she* sound in the wind; the side of a hill covered in razor grass looking like the hide of a giant animal.

Along these roads you had to drive slowly. In the dusk, wallabies could suddenly bound across the road, inches from your car. If you stopped in time they disappeared into the paddocks, and the humps of razor grass all turned into dream creatures. If you hit one it could do big damage to the radiator. *Poor baby* was my mother's mantra every time she passed a squashed thing. "Something should be done about this," she once told me, and I'd snapped back: "It would be a full-time job, traveling up and down, moving the kill off the road." "No," she'd said, "something should be done to protect the animals. You'd think the mother wallabies, and bandicoots, and wombats would tell their babies not to go onto the white streak leading nowhere." As if the babies would've listened.

"Over there's the Suicide Cliffs," the man said.

"Really?"

He nodded. "Mainlanders come down here all the time. They won't do it at home, but they don't mind coming down here and stinking up our water." He lit a cigarette, without opening the window. "They probably think it's their last hurrah, but who'd even notice?"

I cleared my throat. "Were you raised around here?"

"No, the highlands." He smoked awhile, flicking ash in the tray. "My grandfather was a trapper." He laughed. "It was different for him: he used the wire noose, not the bullet."

I skipped a breath. "What was the wire noose?"

"Oh, well, the necker." He exhaled slowly. "Those blokes built traps with anything they could find. Stick a bush pole up a possum tree; place a wire noose halfway along it; the lazy possum, using it as a shortcut, will get caught and jump off the pole." He took one hand off the wheel, and tugged at an imaginary noose. "Incredible. They were canny, the snarers were then; I've seen a dangling loop over a game trail, it'd release with the animal's head in it, spring up, and that's that." He nodded, satisfied. "They'd use old wood, hemp, any bit of wire. My grandfather had the record for the biggest haul of possum skins year after year. He was King of the Snarers."

"It sounds like you learned a lot from him."

"I did," he said, and in a deep voice warned, "'Respect what you take: you are taking something's life.'" Now he sounded angry: "Everyone's out there shooting wallaby for pet food. It's only twenty-five dollars for a bloody license! That's why I'd like to get into the human consumption market."

"Truly?" He was a hunter. I realized in a flash what he hung from the coat racks welded behind us.

"You need to do a special course and then convert your truck. You need to be able to wash the roo down immediately, and you need a refrigerator."

"Like a mobile abattoir."

His glance was quick, expressionless. "It would be bloody

expensive, but it would be worth it. Call the guy with the chilled van, and say, 'I'm starting shooting at seven, meet me at twelve.' I might only shoot twenty, but it's twenty dollars each, and at least I wouldn't have to skin them." He turned to me. "If it's pet food you have to have the animal skun out completely, completely dressed down. And no one now even wants the skins. Even in the eighties you could get fifteen dollars for a good possum skin, maybe six dollars for a wallaby."

The hunter lit another cigarette, and I noticed there was no lever to open my door. "I went out the other night," he continued. "One whole paddock was moving. All you could see was black, moving. Well, I shot forty, in three hours, off one paddock." He flicked ash, looking pleased. Then he smiled at me: our date was going well. "The worst part about this job," he confided, "is you predominantly become a hermit."

"At least you're your own boss."

"Oh, you get peace and quiet." He nodded. "And I've seen things no other human would ever see . . ."

In the distance the beached Mercedes appeared. I felt a wave of relief. "There's my car!" It was squashing a cluster of shrubs, the back wheel raised off the ground. Suddenly, I was embarrassed. Once, driving in the wind, I'd watched a butterfly slaughtered on the Mercedes insignia: a poor wing caught in the inverted peace symbol. It didn't count for anything that this car was actually a wreck; the enormous rusted thing glimmered with false promise in the twilight.

The man stopped the truck. After taking off his seat belt, he suddenly leaned down and pulled something from underneath the seat. I started, but it was only a photo album. "This might interest you."

"Did you take these?" He nodded. They were photographs of deer: a deer staring straight into the camera, a silhouette of a deer's antlers against a sunset. I turned the page and saw photographs of two gray kangaroos fighting in the mist; another of a kangaroo tending her joey. These were the animals the man could've killed had he wanted to. "Taking these photos," I said, "it must be very intimate."

He smiled, staring at my thighs. "It is."

I turned the pages and tried not to show shock. Now there was a series of him, dressed in camouflage, smiling broadly as he squatted over a deer which he'd just shot in the neck. I turned another page. He was underneath that same deer's head in a taxidermy shop. "Yeah, I guess the worst part about this job is you lose all social life," he told me. I kept turning the pages. I thought of the photographs included in true-crime books. I'd seen a naked woman, like a failed magic act, literally severed in two. One half of the woman's body lay in the grass. The other, pelvis tilted upward, had been left next to it. Two fully clothed policemen, both wearing suits and hats, were each crouching over a body half, gazing into the camera.

The man had to let me out because the passenger door was jammed from the inside. There were hills in every direction, but I'd crashed in what seemed the one flat spot. The bags of apples still sat on the chair, but there were no houses nearby. To the east mountains were still illuminated. Trees made abstract marks against the bleached grass. To the west the sun had set: there were just undulating shadows, the sound of waves. A baton was being passed, and the night animals would soon take over. I unlocked the car, opening up the bonnet. It was getting colder, but I didn't want him to see me shiver lest it turn him on. What frightened me most was the sense of his strength and his slumped shoulders. When he straightened up it would be with fury. I watched his hands inside the car. This was the world shutting me out. For all I knew he could take apart every working object in the engine.

"Your fan belt's fucked." He laughed, pulling out a long stretch of rubber. "Has someone got it in for you?"

"You think someone did it deliberately?"

"Well, it looks a bit like it."

"How would you know?"

"Well, you couldn't say for sure."

I took a deep breath. "What seems to be the problem with it?"

"It's been cut with a razor blade, or maybe a sharp pair of scissors." He smiled at me. I thought he was trying to be sympathetic, but then pleasure settled into his expression. "If the fan belt had snapped it would be shredded." He was enjoying himself. He looked down again, still smiling. "Some cunt's also cracked a bleeder."

"I'm sorry?"

"They've cracked the fucking bleeder on your brake caliper. You'll need brake fluid."

Shaking my head, I stared into the engine. The man stood too close and I hoped for an approaching car, half expecting to see Veronica's fingerprints. I started talking softly about my day. I'd heard that made killers less likely to kill. If they knew you better, they'd start identifying with you. You'd remind them of their niece or the girl next door, and although it might piss them off, they couldn't bring themselves to go through with the murder. "The kids in my class came on an excursion here just a few months ago . . ." I began, realizing this "identification" theory was stupid: a lot of people would be thrilled to kill a family member or neighbor. "The kids are nine years old and very sweet, so curious about the world, interested in everything . . ."

"Take off your panty hose."

I stood, openmouthed, staring at him.

He pulled out a knife. "Take off your panty hose, Miss Byrne."

I started to do as he said, my spastic shadow copycatting against the razor grass. I started taking my panty hose off, in a way I hoped was completely asexual. We'd been warned in high school to make ourselves as unattractive as possible in this situation. Try to burp, or even fart, the teacher advised, seem dirty or repellent in some way. I took off my shoes. I pushed the panty hose's elastic waist down, then pulled from the knees.

"Do it behind the Merc."

I walked awkwardly behind the car, the lowered crotch constricting my movement. The road dropped down into a ditch. For miles the grass waved in one direction, then swayed away, changing its mind. Nothing: nothing but a crow making her cow sounds in the wind. I choked back a sob: this was my chance to run, but where to? And now barefoot, how far would I get? I heard him pacing. I struggled to take off the panty hose. He'd smell the sex on them, and go ahead with whatever it was he had planned. I remembered the woman's high-pitched voice: was she trying to warn me? Or merely to stop him from going out and satisfying the urge? Suddenly the truck's huge headlights bathed everything in sulphur. I said a prayer. Then, squinting, I limped slowly back to him. Trying to get out of the light, I handed the panty hose over. He looked at me with his swollen eyes— one animal sensing completely his advantage. He examined the panty hose, pulling them tight. I whimpered as he wrapped the nylon round his fingers. Then with his knife he cut it loudly into strips.

With the spotlight he'd illuminated the engine. He turned from me and bent back under the bonnet. I stood, shocked, watching him. A cool breeze touched at the back of my bare calves. He wrapped the nylon legs around a series of pulleys. "Don't know what you'd have done without yours truly," he said. I couldn't answer; every cunning little platitude had left me. The man didn't care. "You'd have had to eat apples until someone came by, heh?" He laughed. "Sleeping in your car until you heard the banging on the roof." He told the story—that I hadn't heard since primary school—of the father and son driving, the father going for help after the car's breakdown; a maniac waking the son by banging the father's head on the car roof. The hunter told this story like it was his own, then he called me over to look at my new fan belt. The cotton gusset stared back at us: I started to cry. "You must be cold?" When I didn't answer, he added wearily, "I'd get home if I were you. It'll take you a while. You'll have to go slow. Keep your hand on the hand brake."

In the rearview mirror I could see him standing in the middle of the road, watching my car crawling away. Every time I looked back he was still there monitoring our distance. All I wanted was to accelerate. When eventually his spot-lights faded I was still barely able to breathe. Night was falling: a blanket with no edges. Driving in the dark on this road it felt like the world had ended and no other souls, but he and I, had made the cut. I drove on so slowly, tears stream-ing down my cheeks. I hummed a string of notes from the music Thomas had played me. It was stupid heading back to Endport, but I was literally unable to stop. If I could I'd have glued wings together. Instead I said a prayer around each corner, at the crest of every hill, while night creatures sang sweetly, "No!" "Wait!" "Stop, you'll die!"

· MURDER AT BLACK SWAN POINT ·

Missing is such a polite word.

$\mathcal{W}$*arwick Wallaby felt the thirst but it was too dangerous to drink water. He lay under a melaleuca tree, listening as all the leaves whispered rumors, and a light breeze spread the word. "What happened to Margot?" they rustled. "Was the abandoned car a hoax?" The wallaby took his bottle from the hollow, then swigged. "Why couldn't I be given a new coat of fur, and end my days as someone's fat old Labrador? Imagine starting over and going to a place where no one knows you." Warwick drank again. "What a relief to go 'missing,'" he thought. "'Missing' is such a polite word, compared to, say, 'slaughtered,' or 'extinct.'"*

The spirit warmed him. Warwick closed his eyes. He was what was known as a psychic detective: if given one of the victim's personal objects, from a crime scene, he could sometimes imagine this crime in his head, even seeing the gnarled faces of the guilty. Unfortunately nothing belonging to Ellie Siddell had been available, but, with remarkable foresight, a magpie had swiped one of Margot's socks from the Harveys' line.

Now Warwick held the item, bracing himself. "Footsteps. A key turning in a lock. A long road . . ." Shaking, the wallaby reached again for the bottle's nipple. "A slamming of a door. Lamplight." The dregs of gin ran down his throat: he threw the bottle to the ground. Above the kookaburra mocked him, but he ignored this laughter. Already he'd seen too much carnage. His mother shot, his father shot, his seven sisters and brothers shot one night, off one paddock. Other animals had fed from their carcasses. "Why?" He saw this scene too clearly. "Why?"

In the distance was a little gray house: the home of Miss Kate Byrne, the schoolteacher. Warwick bounded toward the picket fence, up the garden path, and ah! there was the lass's garbage bin. He tipped it over, and picked carefully through the refuse for another beverage, just a little something to quench a thirst. It was almost certain a hunter would be waiting by the watering hole; another bastard wanting his balls for a child's coin purse. The wallaby's paws were trembling. He was sweating. Insects seemed to crawl under his fur, and the bird's laughter echoed on and on—a rumor was going round the bush that Warwick's gift was no more than a dole of delirium tremens. "It is not true!" He picked through the garbage, shivering, as the ants moved down his tail.

The wallaby froze. There was the sound of a car approaching; the steady rumble of an oversized German engine. Terrified, he stood clutching at the sock. But "oh so bright!" He was caught in the headlights unable to move! "So very bright!" Nothing in the bush was so bright: his pupils closed down. "Where am I?" he called. Everything appeared in x-ray: white trees grew against a black sky. The trees, burning on his retinas, were outlined in red. In the distance Warwick heard gunshots. "Where am I?" he screamed silently toward the light. "Where?" And then, the sock still in his little paw, he felt his eyes roll back. "A bottle being broken, glass splinters like licks of flame. Blood on white tiles. Blood on the carpet. A car parked by a cliff . . . Oh no!" Warwick saw the face. "Oh no!" He saw the face . . . and it was too horrible!

OUR HOLIDAY HOUSE was the perfect location for a crime photographer. Past the picket fence lay a wooded pathway, dappled with light. It cut through a tangle of shrubbery—convenient for shallow graves—and led to a gray weatherboard house. The house, appropriately weary, slightly slumped, was built just after the war. Not wanting to seem ostentatious, my grandfather had painted it battleship gray. He was an executive at a chemical company and, later, on the eve of retiring, he bought enough of this color on staff discount to sink a fleet. Inside, my grandmother strived for what she imagined to be California chic. She decorated the living room in the fashion of a Perry Mason novel. *The Case of the Moon Jungle Interior.* A flying saucer lamp hovered over a black-hole dining table. Malign potted plants waited in every corner to wrestle you on the orange fireball of a rug. It was not necessary, of course, to go retro to get good crime shots: the interior of any crime scene becomes shabby and dated as soon as the photograph has been taken. Even in black and white the image looks yellowed, as if the corpse's decay had infected the film.

Reaching into my handbag I found the mini-bottle of shampoo and sewing kit I'd pilfered from the hotel. I dumped them on the dining table, then wandered around each room checking that the windows were closed; that no one was hiding in the closets next to the moldering life jackets. *You are safe here, you have always been safe.* In the pantry was the Scotch I bought for Thomas: one shot burned away the taste of cordial but I kept hold of the bottle.

Walking to my bedroom, I turned on the television— people in a sitcom burbled, then laughter. I lay on the single bed, not moving an inch. Slowly I could distinguish gradations of dark. To my left was a sampler my grandmother had worked: little animals in waistcoats jumped around Psalm 33. Above the headboard, another sampler made the plea, *If I should die before I wake I pray thee Lord my soul to take.* I lay still. There were all these extra minutes fear made you alert to. Old houses harbor the most inexplicable creaks and groans. Pouring another glass of Scotch sounded like a gurgling scream; canned laughter, a window smashing. At a certain hour, as dark swelled, ax murderers started growing in the flower beds. Or else Margot did. *You are safe here*, I embroidered. *You are safe here, as you have always been.*

I thought of the odor inside the man's shed—metallic, sweet—it had been the animals he'd had strung up on the other side of the wall. Through the fly wire, his workroom must have been attached to a drying shed. It was no wonder there had been flies everywhere. I had stood stupidly on the animals' skins while meters away hung their carcasses. I could still smell them. Perhaps it was on my clothes or in my hair. I sniffed at my shirt, then stood up and stripped. Holding the bottle, I walked toward the bathroom. The telephone rang— I froze. My heart was beating fast. I closed my eyes; to the sound of each ring, I wailed, "No!"

Veronica had two modes. She cultivated all that languid ennui to hide pure cunning. I had seen her overwhelmed by murderous thoughts: Veronica with bright, bright eyes, all caffeinated like a jerky little bird. She had despised me from the moment we'd met. I'd been ridiculously naive. On that excursion, just as I had been studying her, she had been studying me; her every compliment, her every kindness, dosed to some precise formula. Veronica had known we were at the hotel and had returned early from her book tour, cutting the fan belt and brakes. She'd wanted me badly frightened, but not hurt. At least, not hurt yet. Veronica had plans for me. After all, she had written her own textbook on how to kill one's rival. The phone kept ringing.

I pictured Thomas and Veronica playing out the Harveys' roles: An adulterer in a finely cut suit walked through the door of his family home and greeted his wife, who was suspicious, who had been suspicious for a long time. His wife demanded the truth. The man was tired from his fucking or tired from his lying, and thought, You want to know? "Yes," he told her. "Of course I am having an affair, of course I am." His wife grabbed a wine bottle, hitting him. He stood there stunned; she cried. He didn't think to call his girlfriend.

They pulled a chair into the bathroom and he sat down while she touched his wound with warm wet cotton wool. She'd caught him having his fun, he'd been punished, and now she was fixing up her little boy. Lying just underneath his anger was his sense he was ridiculous: he would never get away from her. They went to bed and lay next to each other. His head throbbed. She started to cry again, but he figured she'd gotten the anger out of her system. He held out his hand. She would not take it. He retracted the hand and waited on his side of the bed, eager for annihilatory sleep.

"How would you feel," I'd once asked Thomas directly, "if your wife were to murder me?" We were lying next to each other in the spare room. For a moment he'd been silent. "I'd put my head in my hands and think: *Kill me! I did it!* And that's what Harvey would've been thinking: *Why didn't she kill me? The bitch slept next to me. She could've driven a knife into my chest! She could have taken scissors to my dick!*" Thomas paused. "Although if someone was sitting on top of me, holding scissors, and it occurred to her to go off and kill some little slut, which would I choose?" He turned to look at me. "Let me get back to you on that."

The telephone stopped. I stared at it another minute before ripping the plug from the wall. Veronica had forsaken all goodness. She was so amoral she thought of this terrorizing as her art; as the purest form of self-expression. I remembered another time, asking Thomas, "You don't think Margot survived?" "Absolutely. And now she's drinking a cocktail." "Wouldn't it be cocoa?" "No," he'd warned gnomically. "You can't be sophisticated *and* virtuous."

I walked into the bathroom. My legs were scratched. I could still smell meat. It could have been in my hair. It could have been on my skin. I poured sweet gunk into the bathwater, then looked up. A fluorescent tube was over the mirror. I searched my face for traces of doom.

Inside all the true-crime books were the same photographs. Publishers must have recycled them, knowing we were all secretly physiognomists. They'd found the ultimate photograph of a murder victim in her school uniform which they reused over and over, alternating others from their *doomed girl* series. There was a shot of doomed girl sunbathing, one hand raised to shield her eyes from the sun as she laughed into the camera. Blowing out candles on a birthday cake, doomed girl was surrounded by the kids with whom she did volunteer work. It was perverse; newspapers chose the prettiest photos, as if any witness would recognize the victim who didn't have her face squashed against a car window, gun to head. Maybe the appeal, for young male readers, was that *they* could've saved them. Or, that they could've killed them. For young women, doomed girls are annoying. It's a reminder one should start locking the doors of the car. A photo of a schoolgirl with bangs and a dental brace stands for never walk home alone on an ill-lit street.

I saw myself still wearing the black underwear that had gotten me into this trouble in the first place. Shivering, I took it off. "I'll go away," I whispered. "I'll go away anywhere. I'll leave this town and head straight to the mainland." I checked the water temperature. The main reason for not leaving immediately was my class. I would break it off with Thomas, but I'd put so much into teaching those kids. I hadn't fulfilled all the goals I'd had.

The sigh on entering the bath: the relief of it. I didn't swim as often now; if I did I'd be overwhelmed by sadness. "I've missed you," I'd say aloud, but then in a second the yearning passed and I didn't even remember what it was I'd lost. Fear, I realized, had made me slightly numb. Walking down the street I sometimes had trouble smiling at people. I would see them coming and think, In thirty seconds look up and smile. In ten seconds. Get ready: smile, you must smile.

The expressions on people's faces betrayed how odd they found me. "Kate, are you all right?" the teachers asked. "You seem jumpy." "Oh, I'm fine," I'd answer. But I had barely any flight mechanism, and my fright wasn't too good either. It's called counterphobia when you rush headlong into the thing that frightens you the most. It can feel a little like not caring: quicksand one sashays toward.

I lay back and bubbles surrounded my neck as would a white fur stole. The Scotch bottle rested on the soap stand. I felt like a woman who knew about the world. Taking slow sips, I applied all my experience to Ellie's situation: Graeme had probably told her his marriage had been on the rocks long before her arrival on the scene. In fact he'd told her he and his wife were thinking of separating, they were discussing it.

I bet Margot sometimes came into the clinic acting as if Ellie wasn't doing a very good job. Margot would look at her meanly, as if thinking, Soon you'll be this old, and Ellie always wanted to answer aloud, "No, I won't." She had started planning to go overseas. She wanted to go backpacking with the money she'd saved working at the clinic. Ellie had come to realize she had been very naive: she could barely even read her old diary entries, because she'd drawn pages of wedding dresses with embroidered trains. She'd designed a bridesmaid's dress and had written down flowers for a bouquet. Nearly a year after moving to Black Swan Point she realized she'd been crazy. Nothing was going to change. She'd been crazy. In the office Ellie made a show of reading postcards from her friends overseas. She ripped certain pages from her diary: it was embarrassing to have ever been so young.

Like in this house, everything in Ellie's house was probably exactly as it was when she was growing up: the daddy longlegs doing yogic stretches on the bathroom ceiling, the tap water tasting like twigs. When she opened the closets' sighing doors, zephyrs of melancholy blew her hair back. Each shelf was like purgatory for all things once loved. Long-punctured inflatable canoes lived next to ancient electric blankets with rusted insides. There were jigsaw puzzles, all of the most inscrutable, infuriating images; and board games missing crucial pieces. *Cluedo* had one murder weapon left; tooth floss was the rope; a paper clip, the lead pipe. In the evenings, when she was small, her family played parlor games, snakes and ladders, gin rummy. Once she and her cousins made their own Ouija board and held a séance with her father. "Who last farted?" they asked the spirits gleefully and the impudent glass spelled out his name.

I stood up for a moment and turned out the light. The water again became still, but for the hot tap's slow drip. I tried not to think of Margot leaving her sleeping husband, then driving through the night. Sometimes I pictured it so clearly I couldn't get to sleep . . .

Ellie's father had probably called all winter to check she had enough firewood. Even though she never lit fires. Even though she didn't know how to. He'd call up, and talk her through the lighting process. And she'd say, "Yes, I've arranged the kindling now, in a tepee, yes . . . Oh! There it goes. It's really raging!" Then she'd hang up, and turn on the radiator. The house looked just the same, but she didn't fit inside it anymore. It shouldn't have had to witness this behavior. Everything the same and her so different. On bad days she got the sense it might blackmail her.

"I find it hard to get aroused," her lover had complained, "surrounded by so many photos of prizewinning marlin." And she'd felt like answering: "Is that all that bothers you? Look underneath the fish photos. Can't you see? Right there on the couch . . . it's my father! My father may as well be sitting very straight, watching television with the volume down, because it's *less excruciating.*" Her lover was pulling off her shirt, with his back to the TV. He couldn't see the documentary on unsolved mysteries that was playing, and when the blurry footage of the Loch Ness Monster appeared—that famous image of a long-necked creature in thick fog—he was running his fingers along her spine, and only she could hear her indignant father calling, "It was probably just a duck!"

Her lover started to whisper the crudest things. Didn't he realize her mother was still in the kitchen? If you squinted you could see her staring into the fridge with a slightly furrowed brow, realizing there was no food. One of her paperbacks was waiting on the countertop, as she took the last orange from the fruit bowl, cut it, and gave half to her husband, offering her daughter a quarter and saving the remaining quarter for herself. *Why does Dad always get half?* Ellie thought as her lover undid his belt, and then his trousers. And then she was shocked. She was shocked for them as he exposed himself, slowly stroking his erection. *Why don't we just cut the orange into thirds?*

He'd push her shoulders gently and she'd fall to her knees, eye level with his gut. A small, round gut from living well. He was grimacing, as if concentrating on impossible calculus, his brow wrinkled into a π symbol. These facial contortions made him the ugliest man in the world. He had the ugliest face you could ever see. He'd start moaning and she had to close her eyes in order to concentrate. Then he'd gently stroke her hair, before pushing her head closer to his crotch. She tried not to gag. "Oh Lord!" Apparently chiropractors see a lot of women who've stuffed up their jaws from doing this sort of thing. "Do you like this?" he would moan, although obviously it was difficult to answer. Did she like *what*? Did she like that her parents were, in fact, all over the house? No. No, she didn't. Their marriage hung in the bathroom like a scratchy old towel; like a shelf of aging sunscreen bottles, the nuptial smell was overwhelming.

Afterwards when he was gone, she wanted to call up her mother, and for her mother to say, nearly in a baby voice, "How's my little girl? How's my sweetheart?" Busy with her own deceit, Ellie didn't realize that in no time her lover's wife would leave him sleeping and drive through the night to pay a visit. She heard her mother's voice and she wished she were nine years old sitting by the fire, burning a piece of paper's edges to make an antique treasure map. She wished she would be sent to bed before *The Sound of Music*'s finale, because it was almost ten o'clock. She wanted to go out into the garden when the guests arrived with a lit sparkler to do her "sparkler dance." And for them all to clap when she came back inside, triumphant.

The push-pull of children and parents separating: a minute ago she had been walking barefoot between her mother and father, watching as their shadows took turns carrying her shoes. Nowadays she sat with them as they came inside from the beach. She watched as they took off their sandals, as they wiped the sand off their skin, and thought, I know too much about your feet. And, I suppose, you know too much about mine. I know too much about the language of your face. And you know too much about the way to say my name. We're like castaways, you and I—families are like castaways on a makeshift raft; baling out water, plugging leaks with whatever we can find—but you'd better teach me again how to swim. I'll kick hard, while strong arms hold me in the water. If I curl up at your feet, pretending to be a baby, perhaps you'll never die.

Margot moved around the Siddells' house, staring at the blank night windows. Her footsteps were heavier on the ground than she'd expected. There was a knife in her pocket for protection. She would teach that girl a lesson; she'd like to cut her pretty face to teach her a lesson. Margot kept each step steady. The wind through the leaves made its whispering and she kept each step steady. Her husband wouldn't cope a day without her. Imagine Graeme putting his big hand into their daughters' little pockets. Shoving in his hand to find a shell before the wash. His fingers would jam against the soft lining, the silky lining. He'd nearly rip the fine stitching, searching as if for a love note wedged into the little fold.

Following the side fence, Margot found a window with a tease of open curtain like a slit of a skirt from ankle to waist. Inside glowed a dull light. She didn't bother with the front door. She walked further, and tried the fly-wire screen around the back. In one dream moment it wheezed open. From the hallway she made her way toward the light. Margot heard breathing. And then a lamp on the bedside table showed off the sleeping girl. The girl breathed in and out.

Her dance dress was hanging on the back of the door. A little slip of velvet which would barely cover her arse. A skinny little dress she'd probably worn for him. *You vain bitch, dancing round the room for my husband, stripping off your slut clothes.* Cold was being injected into Margot's veins. Cold was surging to her brain. She walked toward the bed. She hated the flutter of the sleeping girl's breath. *Everything you see belongs to me.* She could feel the knife pierce the skin, the young unblemished skin. The mouth was gasping, spluttering a half scream, and Margot wanted it to stop. *Every time you laugh, that's my happiness. When he kisses you, when he puts his fingers inside you: that's love you've stolen from me.* As Margot brought the knife down, she knew she was also dying. *Stop spluttering.* Her hands were covered in the girl's blood, and she could already feel herself plunging, she could feel her body falling. Her hands were covered in warm blood and she thought, *It's you who's killing me. Stop spluttering.*

The bathwater had turned cold. I lifted myself out, heavy. Sand, on the floorboards, stuck to my feet. Sand was sprinkled through the sheets; it was in the rug by the bed. Brushing the grit away, I lay down—eyes closed, heart horizontal—playing at some ideal of night, while outside a dog refined its barking. Before she drifted away, the girl must have thought that nothing could happen, nothing would happen. *Sleep the sleep of the just babes.* In the morning, early, she planned to get up and start again. So, *lie there still*, she heard her mother's voice whisper. *Lie there still. Close your eyes. The window will cover you in a sheet of moonlight, while I tell you this story.*

All the old concerns flooded back.

Terence Tiger paced up and down, lecturing. It was important the younger animals understood that humans have essentially four main blood groups. "Type A, B, O, and AB," *he explained slowly.* "Then, to further individualize blood stains, polymorphic enzymes are analyzed. These provide pathologists with subgroups known as the PGM or phosphoglucomutase types." *The tiger paused, wondering if the smaller-brained marsupials could keep up.* "It was determined that Ellie Siddell's ABO blood type was A PGM 1, and Graeme's was A PGM 2-1. There was no sample of Margot's blood, but according to hospital records from when Margot was delivering her three daughters, it was ascertained that she had type O blood."

The tiger glanced down, checking that he held the little beasts' attention. Kitty Koala, on a nearby branch, nodded and he continued. Using a twig, Terence drew a rough sketch of the Siddells' floor plan in the dirt. He traced a stick figure lying by her stick bed, and all the old concerns flooded back: was this fascination with true crime not slightly crass? A way of fetishizing death? Of making it as kitsch as possible? All too often, Terence worried, this supposed analysis of the criminal mind had no methodology: we're just ghoulish Victorians "studying" a hanged man's death mask. He drew a stick refrigerator—it was amazing how such a ubiquitous white good could look so sinister. Often murderers used their fridges and, yes, also their washing machines for such grisly purposes . . . the tiger cleared his throat.

"According to the forensic evidence gathered by the police," he continued, "the only place Eleanor Siddell bled was in her house. Predictably, type A PGM 1 blood was found all over her bedclothes and mattress. Her undergarments were soaked in her blood, as were a large section of the carpet and the items lying on this carpet, including her nurse's uniform.

"There was also a series of bloody handprints on the north wall of the hallway, as if the killer had leaned in, trying to steady him- or herself. The killer proceeded to the bathroom, washed his or her hands, then flicked them dry against the white bathtub, hence these pinkish streaks." Terence looked once again at Kitty. "Now, pathologists found type A blood on the girl's nightgown and the knife discovered near her body. However,"

Terence paused, "the PGM subgrouping on these items could not be determined."

All the little animals squirmed, not realizing this information's significance.

"What are you suggesting?" Kitty Koala asked knowingly.

The tiger stared at the crudely drawn map. He tapped the twig against his hind leg, stifling a howl. "Technically, it's possible that Graeme Harvey's blood was also on the dead girl's nightshirt, and the knife found beside her body . . ."

WAKING FELT LIKE another car crash: I opened my eyes and the day, too bright, came screeching toward me. It seemed I had woken in someone else's dream. Closing my eyes again, I burrowed further into the bedclothes—if I went back to sleep perhaps I would be safe. "But what if this is a dream, and when you dream it's not a dream?" Anaminka asked calmly one day, setting off an hour of intense debate. In some ways her question was further along than Philosophy 101's "How do I know if I am dreaming?" For the answer is: you don't actually know. It's not logically impossible that the whole of life is a dream, and Anaminka had asked, "If in fact we are dreaming, then what are dreams?" If life is a dream, and in that dream we go to sleep, at that moment are we dead? No one, neither scientists nor philosophers, knows why we dream. What if children's terror of night and night monsters is just their connecting the dots between dreaming and death?

> Billy: *Life could be like one big dream, like everyone's dreams put together. You've just gone into a never-ending sleep when you were in your mum's tummy, then you come out, and you have a dream about your life, and then you wake up and you're dead.*

Darren: *I would be dead now, because in my dreams I've fallen off about fifty cliffs.*
Eliza: *Usually you know when you're not dreaming because you can fly in your dreams.*
Lucien: *But I've been left with the question, "Have I really flown out of my bed?" And I don't know. Sleepflying is what I've thought I've been doing, but the thing is I've never been looking out of my eyes. There's a mini helicopter watching me. I'm looking at myself without a mirror.*

The light through the curtain's edges pried me from my bed. The light was so strong it stripped everything bare. It was so bright the wallaby grass outside could look snow-capped. Our garden used to be in near-constant darkness—a huge cypress had hovered over us like a dull-green mushroom cloud, and with so little sun, no native plants could grow underneath. After my grandparents passed away, my parents had the tree cut down. When the chain saw started my mother had to draw the curtains. She couldn't watch. The stink of wood chip seeped through every room. Later, after the sunburned logger had finished his deafening work, I walked out into the garden fearful of seeing a toppled nest. The ground was carpeted with sawdust, and logs lay about. My father stood sadly in the middle of the wreckage, sun flooding down, and he turned to me, warning, "Avoid the heart." The logger had told him that if you cut into the heart of the wood, the tree "shits itself." It shatters into thousands of splinters and the timber is no good to anyone.

After the tree left, a strange comedy began. My parents

called in a professional house mover. He sawed the weather-board house in half, employing two forklift trucks to simultaneously move each half to a better vantage point (perhaps when the house had been built the sea was considered too wild to view from one's window). The house was restumped and rewired, closer to the cliff, on the site of the cypress. The last tins of discounted paint were used to reanoint the exterior. For a few weeks afterward, the locals would come of an evening, standing outside our home and staring as though it were a natural wonder.

My head throbbed. I wasn't used to drinking, and I moved around slowly, the princess of dumb. This was the moment I needed my wits about me, but as I drew the curtains each picture seemed very wrong. During the night the house had taken off again, relanding with each angle out. It would have been no less strange to discover the house had swum to the bottom of the sea, than finding, over and over, the grand, stern cypress gone. No less strange than looking out the window in the mornings, realizing each view had been swapped, and I was living alone. My mother was not standing in an enormous sun hat whispering to her new saplings: "We're so glad you're in our garden. What a lovely plant you are." My father was not chopping the leftover cypress, his tall thin frame negotiating a short stump of log. While I'd had my head dunked in my own illusions, all the comforts of the past had stood up and left. Living away from home, there was no one to tell me who I was anymore. Now I was *looking at myself without a mirror*. I didn't have their ideas in which to see my reflection. I had got lost in someone else's life.

Alastair: *If someone kicks you in a dream, you can't feel it.*
Henry: *If someone shoots you, you can't feel it.*
Alastair: *And sometimes if someone has a knife, and they're threatening to kill you, in a dream you can't stop them stabbing you, but then you wake up.*
Lucien: *Or else you go to sleep again.*

I went to the kitchen to find a knife. It seemed I should take some precautions, but the cutlery drawer only mocked me. Everything was from the 1960s, now rusting or broken. Dozens of corks had collected there for no apparent reason.

Slamming the drawer, something occurred to me. Thomas might have rejected the notion Veronica was psychotic. But Lucien had not. I thought of the morbid portrait he'd drawn of his mother: a strange psychic record of her rage. He had been trying to warn me and I'd approached the situation with perfect myopia. Riffling through my textbooks, I'd been hungry for any information on children's art. What, I'd wondered, was he trying to say? Drawings could be symbolic expressions of a child's perception of the world: shy and depressed children, I'd read, had the tendency more often to draw tiny figures, to omit the mouth, the nose, and the eyes, and to cut off hands; while by contrast aggressive children tended to draw long arms, big hands, teeth, and genitals. Children with psychosomatic complaints more often showed clouds; children who stole more often shaded the hands; obese children drew figures taking up an unusually large area of their page. And the children of true-crime writers? I'd hopelessly searched further.

In one book's appendix there was a measure to test the drawings of children in distress. It had seemed complicated. You scored the drawing if the child had included fruit trees, but not if these trees were pine trees, coconut trees, or palm trees. You scored the drawing if the child had drawn an enclosed figure, even if this enclosure was a house. You scored it if the enclosed figure's hands were cut off, even if they were only in pockets. Then, after you'd calculated your score, you were supposed to ask a series of questions. For example: "What's the worst thing that's ever happened to you?" If the child said, "Nothing," you were then supposed to say, breezily, "Oh, everyone has something bad that happens."

I dragged a chair toward a higher kitchen cupboard, looking for something sharp. If I were more resourceful I could have booby-trapped this whole house. There were candles, and old rubber gloves; scraps of chicken wire, sandpaper, nails, and a hacksaw. Foreign objects, relating to the natural world, made their way into all the house's corners. At one stage I'd found the ceiling stained, and had supposed the roof to be leaking. A local handyman came over and looked up thoughtfully. "Not to worry," he'd reassured me, "it's just possum piss." I now leaned forward. The cupboard smelled dank. I leaned forward again, and felt my face covered in cobwebs. I had found my father's fishing basket; and after wiping free the cobwebs, inside it, I found the knife.

Anaminka: *You know how I said, "What are dreams made of?" I've found a solution. There's a little factory in heaven that's making dreams. And this*

dream is about a lion and it eats you, do you want it?
Okay, then this is a dream about chocolate . . . But you
have to pay. You pay in nightmares.
Lucien: *In all my dreams it's mute, in every dream I*
haven't spoken.
Lucien: *In all my dreams I can't see anyone's face. I can't*
see any details. I see color. But I don't see who they
are. I know someone's there, but I don't see their faces.

I too had known someone was there. And last night, driving in the dark, I had finally seen their face. Veronica's malice was hardly a surprise. But Thomas could no longer claim innocence. I stepped down from the chair, examining the knife.

At first I'd felt uncomfortable talking to the children about death, even though for them it was an area of intense interest. Younger children recognized the fact of physical death, but could not separate it from life: they'd take off their doll's limbs, and realign them in mutant poses; they'd lie on the floor, playing extinct, and scream for a Life injection. These young ones couldn't conceive that death was a permanent condition, ironically, because it seemed too great a force. Death could eat and it could drink. So surely Death could be outtricked and outrun. "Do you think of Death often?" a famous psychologist once asked a smart four-year-old. "Yes, I think of when I hit it on the head, and yet it doesn't go away." Around my children's age, some difficult lessons were about to be learned. The day before they'd had to face the fact that the animals, with which they'd identified, had been unable to outwit mortality.

Lucien's parents had probably drilled this message in early. I thought of something I'd witnessed at the school fair. Children bearded with chocolate icing had surrounded the cupcake-decorating table. Balloons were being twisted: "Choose between a sausage dog or a saber!" From a distance I'd noticed Thomas and Lucien by the horror table. In a row were a series of black cardboard boxes. The eyeballs box contained peeled grapes; the guts box, red jelly. Cheese sticks were the corpse's waxy fingers, spaghetti the hair. I'd watched Lucien grimacing as he put his hands in with the severed ears—dried apricots—and had felt chaos at work. Thomas was encouraging his son's familiarity with the butchered body. "How does it feel?" he would have asked the little boy. "Describe the texture to me: do you find it soft? too soft? Concentrate. Does it give to the touch?" I now wondered whom he had been imagining was lying there dissected.

Carrying the knife, I walked to my bedroom and opened the wardrobe. I knew I had to approach Thomas directly. At midday Lucien had Junior League cricket. I would take the car to the garage, then give Thomas an ultimatum: "Stop this!" I would yell, "or I'll leave town! I'll finish teaching your child, and all the others!" I opened the wardrobe and looked through my clothes. Everything seemed so dowdy. Thomas said he liked the way I dressed: it was probably the antithesis of his wife's style, but I wanted to confront him with more sophistication. I held up a shirt with a low neckline, posing.

The great irony, I realized, was that all the locals fervently believed Graeme Harvey killed Eleanor Siddell. I had not believed it. In a small town people tell stories for every other reason than communicating truth. I didn't think Ellie was with another man that night; nor in the end that Graeme waited for the man to leave, then killed her in a jealous rage. I didn't think Margot's shoes were found on the edge of the cliff; nor that Graeme had planted them there, hoping to suggest she'd jumped straight out of her slippers into the waves below. In a small town people will tell stories they don't believe themselves. The school receptionist had explained to me: "If you have a horrible, violent psychopath who kills a body, and slashes it up, and smears blood everywhere, well, if he comes home and he has a little budgerigar in a cage, and he puts his big bloody mitt in the cage, and strokes the bird, oh-so-gently, well that makes what he's done so much more awful. It doesn't have to be a bird, though," she'd said sincerely. "It can be a cat or a dog he pets, any animal! And after all, this man was a vet!"

There had been an obituary notice for Graeme Harvey in the local newspaper a few weeks ago. He'd died of throat cancer, which is apparently a vicious way to die. It starts with a terrible cough, one's neck becomes swollen, one finds it hard to eat and so starves. The notice was very simple. It didn't mention Margot. It didn't mention Ellie. It didn't mention how strange people initially found his decision to stay in Black Swan Point. The hidden meaning of "he served the community with great dedication" was that, after his wife's disappearance, he'd continued working at the veterinary clinic where he'd met his young mistress and conducted the affair. Maybe if you stayed in the same place, all the toxicity, eventually, was neutralized: the road she was murdered on became just another road; the day she went missing, just another day. Perhaps staying in Black Swan Point was his only choice. It was the way to prove he'd not been dreaming a bad dream, the way to avoid having to explain why he was a widower. Imagine moving away, still knowing there was this place, like a blood clot always marring your vision. Here, *life was as it always had been and never was.*

I picked out a long floral dress, thinking of Graeme Harvey. That poor man. Measuring guilt on an island settled foremost as a prison was bound to be sensitive. By blaming Ellie's death on Graeme, Margot got to be just a nice lady who possibly disappeared. Perhaps our fantasy about her innocence was a fantasy about our own innocence. I'd once watched a bride and groom posing, with a horse-drawn carriage, outside the convict-built prison for their wedding photographs; they weren't being ironic about marriage, it was just the jail was our most scenic location. The walls of the prison, made of old sandstone, were beautiful. And this was the way we reinvented ourselves. We sweetened history by making fudge on the site of the brutal Female Factory; we painted a gravestone white to hide its convict stain.

I slipped on the dress. It was green cotton, nearly sheer, with a rose-sprig print and buttons running all the way up the front. I should have worn a petticoat underneath, but I'd be careful not to stand in direct sunlight. In the bathroom mirror I applied lipstick, quite a deep red lipstick, then eye makeup. Affecting my startled look, I put on the eyeliner and shadow and mascara. Through the looking glass, this was what was on the other side: more looking glasses. A million tiny pieces of mirror.

Darren: *If you were in a dream, and you got in a fight
and had your head kicked off, you could pick it up and
screw it back on again.*
Henry: *You could play head soccer.*
Lucien: *If you played football with your head you'd
actually be at an advantage, because your eyes would
be like a camera and you could tell if it hit the post or
not.*
Alastair: *The only bad thing about that is, you wouldn't
look so good after everyone had been kicking you
around.*
Danielle: *You'd look better.*

I finished making up my face and sighed. There was a
blind spot in *Murder at Black Swan Point.* The locals' gossip
was not totally without basis. The forensic evidence had been
confusing, and perhaps could not completely exonerate Dr.
Harvey. Pathologists didn't analyze any of the items gathered
from the crime scene until almost a month after Ellie Siddell's death. Then they took the collected matter out of the
plastic bags, and tried to determine which blood belonged to
the three people believed to have bled at the time surrounding the murder. Not surprisingly, Ellie's blood type was found
all over her house. The bloodstains on her underpants and
nightgown, however, were too difficult to subgroup. Pathologists could only confirm the blood to be type A: both Ellie's
and Graeme's blood type. In Dr. Harvey's defense, proteins
in biological matter can deteriorate quickly, leaving further
categorization impossible.

What was significant, Thomas had explained to me, was

that blood type O, most probably Margot's blood, had been found on a blue hand towel in the Siddells' bathroom, and on paper tissues in the abandoned station wagon. This suggested that in all probability she had bled at the Siddells', and had then driven away still bleeding in the car. But even Thomas would agree, off the record, that given the scale of brute violence, if Margot was the murderer, she'd left remarkably few traces. There was a famous theory in criminal detection, the exchange theory: just as a criminal leaves traces at a site, so they take them when they go. Experts would have expected that whoever killed Eleanor Siddell so savagely would have been covered in her blood. None of Ellie's blood was found on the car's upholstery. Criminologists were also puzzled by the way this crime of passion—the vandalized room, slashed clothes, and frenzied knife blows—seemed to have been so cleanly and methodically dealt with. No fingerprints were found at the site, not even on the bloodied knife, nor on the taps in the kitchen and bathroom.

You might conclude that, even in moments of homicidal rage, Margot was a stickler for cleanliness, were it not for the forensics inside the Harveys' house. Blood type O, again possibly Margot's blood, was inexplicably found on the bedroom carpet and on a rug in the bathroom. Investigators had initially assumed these stains were due to Dr. Harvey bleeding after the bottle blow. It was not until the investigation was all but over that pathologists established some of these stains also matched Margot's blood type. Graeme claimed to have no idea how his wife had come to bleed in the exact same place. Had she visited him after Ellie's murder? Had she tried to take her own life in the house where her children were sleeping? Graeme was first questioned while badly con-cussed, but in the weeks that followed he remembered noth-ing new. Apparently he was suffering great shock. Overnight he had lost his wife and his lover, and was left on his own to raise three young daughters.

I closed my eyes to stop the spinning. I vowed to cut Thomas from my heart, although apparently desire would not go away immediately, in fact the reverse. I was glad the outfit I'd chosen was so flattering. Wearing such a delicate dress, I didn't want to haul around my usual handbag. In my parents' bedroom was the tea chest that I'd once raided for dressing up. Opening it, I found a hundred beautiful things. I pulled out a beaded evening purse: a kingfisher was sewn on one side.

People always tell you, over and over, in the most stern, boring way, "you have to pay." How unfortunate that they are right, and how surprising to have no influence over the price. "Yes, yes, I will pay, I will, but I'll pay *later*; and I'll pay in some way that's still a wee bit fun for me." I needed to be careful with Thomas. I could no longer trust him. All his sweetness meant nothing when held up to this great negli-gence.

Jamming the knife into the evening purse I thought of Dr. Harvey. That poor man. Later, he never talked to journalists about his first marriage, or its dramatic conclusion. In some ways he should've spoken; his silence was taken as a sign of haughtiness, which, in Tasmania, was taken as a sign of guilt. Perhaps people were quick to point the finger at him, because they felt his wife had not; she had punished the young girl for the affair, whereas he was far from innocent. Even if he hadn't lifted a finger, they said, he'd contributed to Ellie's death.

Graeme Harvey on the day he went back to work: he turned the key in the lock and entered the reception area Ellie had tended like their living room. The office seemed cleaner than he had remembered it, the carpet a lighter shade of blue. Her cardigan was on the back of her work chair. There was a list on her desk in a shorthand she must have invented; half the time, he couldn't understand what she'd been planning to do. He opened her desk drawer, saw a wad of coupons, and closed it again. Magazines were fanned out on the coffee table: they would be missing all the competition entry forms. He imagined Ellie cutting out every coupon thinking, *Something's going to happen. Something's going to happen to me.*

The couch in the reception area was old and it was leather. It needed to be replaced. The last time he'd come back to work, after two weeks off for school holidays, before he'd done anything, before even opening one letter, he had locked the clinic's door, then he'd undressed her from the waist down, placing her on the couch. Ellie thought it was dirty. She didn't like her skin touching this dirty thing everyone had brushed up against. As he fucked her she barely even moved. He'd spent two weeks away. The less she moved the rougher he became. He hurt her like he had the first time, when she'd barely even known how to move underneath him: her arse and thighs like splayed butterfly wings. Off and on, for the rest of the afternoon, she'd cried. She said she was upset because her skin had touched this dirty thing, the couch. Later, he realized she was angry at his leaving; staying still to test whether he'd even noticed.

By the time Graeme Harvey got home from work the baby-sitter had fed his daughters, but he still had to put them to bed. He read three books every night. Each girl chose one book. They were about dogs with supernatural powers, or princesses who are kissed and come back to life. The girls took turns turning the pages. After he read to them, they had to brush their teeth. The elder girls were okay. But the youngest, the four-year-old, wanted to turn the taps on and off by herself. She'd stand by the sink on the yellow plastic stool, holding a cartoon toothbrush covered in strawberry-flavored toothpaste. She'd dip the toothbrush in and out of her mouth, to little effect. Then, sitting on the toilet, she would advise him on how it was best to wipe.

He tried to put the littlest girl to bed. She claimed that her toys couldn't get to sleep. So he sang, a talk-singing, to the animals lining her bed. He wondered who could see him trying to pacify a battered old lamb, singing: *Go to sleee-p, go to sleee-p, go to sleeep little shee-eep;* holding his daughter in his arms, keeping her head and neck safe in the crook of his arm, safe rocking back and forward, trying to put her to sleep. "You're my cradle," she said. Her body was tiny in the pajamas. When it seemed she was tiring, he put her head on the pillow and covered her with the sheet. "Lie next to me," the little girl said. But he lay on the carpet next to her bed; a corner of light covering his feet. He'd been leaving lights on around the house. Leaving doors open so that the lights could be seen. Remembering each night which lights and which doors correlated: the delicate mathematics of fear control.

Lying on the floor he remembered his dead lover's body: her skin; her taste; the blemishes only he knew. Ellie would leave the back door open so he could visit whenever he chose. Sometimes he would visit early in the morning, finding her desperate not to leave her bed. She would moan, pained by the effort of bringing herself to consciousness—it was such hard work having to open those eyes. "Oh yes," he'd say, when finally she looked at him. "Oh yes, I love the way you suffer in the morning."

The little girl, lying in bed, told him she was hungry. He brought her a slice of apple. She said she was thirsty. She got water in a sippy cup. And finally he was annoyed. "I'm going to get angry in a minute. I want you to lie still, and close your eyes, and go to sleep." He coaxed her to lie down once more, to put her head on the pillow, but she was still all wriggling energy. He spread out the blue cotton sheet above her and let the air catch underneath so as it fell lightly on top of her, the blue sheet rippled. "Look, I'm underwater!" the girl squealed. She was laughing, enjoying the breeze of the soft sheet. "Do it again! Do it again!" And so he lifted the sheet up into the air and suddenly he noticed his youngest daughter shared her mother's smile; an ungainly smile that took over her whole face. What would happen when she bled through her night-gown and learned about blood the way her mother had? "Do it again," she squealed, throwing up her little arms and legs. She was laugh-smiling, and he drowned her again. *Rock me the sea, rock me and send me to the deep depths of sleep.*

THESE APPARITIONS were on suburban ovals every-where. They wore white T-shirts, white trousers, and white canvas hats as protection from the sun. They had just advanced from plastic bats and balls to the real thing. Some of them held the wooden cricket bat, and when the hard ball approached ducked out of sight. Others stood poised to make a hit, but—as if the bat was a propeller—missed, and spun around 360 degrees. If the bat made contact with the ball it was quite an achievement. The kids cheered and the batsman was encouraged to run; there was the tangle of skinny limbs as he hobbled, all protective pads, down the wicket and back again. The boys' bowling, similarly unortho-dox, then drew focus. The bowler, as he was running, might suddenly remember to hitch up his trousers. He'd then raise his arm, without having yet learned to release the ball on the apex, and it would be a lollipop: a slow throw up, up, then down, down, in a moping parabola. Rarely did anyone catch the hard ball, especially not the fielders. The fielders raised their hands in shrinking prayer. They genuflected as the ball hurtled toward them; squinting, or even closing their eyes, as if facing an approaching eclipse.

Panning out there was a crew of fathers umpiring, or sitting on foldout chairs keeping score. Other fathers stood, arms crossed, watching the game. What would be the appropriate term for this group? *A frown of fathers. A spanking of daddies. A nymph's dozen.* They'd worked all week, and now gave the little boys their undivided attention.

Thomas was standing right at the very edge of the oval. Possibly he enjoyed cricket more than Lucien did. I strode toward him, the dress smooth against my body. Averting my eyes, I tried to pass a group of fathers, but Mr. Stackhouse intercepted me. He was a swarthy man with broad hands, and he wore a T-shirt bearing the message: *It doesn't matter who wins or loses but who gets most pissed at the end of the game.* He was talking to Henry Ledder's dad. Mr. Ledder was charming in a thuggish way with a handsome, if slightly fat, face. I imagined he had a temper. (During Show and Tell Henry had told us about a video of his father's recent fishing trip. Mr. Ledder and friends had filmed themselves driving hired cars, very fast, in second gear down gravel roads, slowing only to shoot stop signs full of bullets.)

"Heard you've had trouble with your car," Mr. Ledder said slowly, not taking his eyes off my dress. News traveled here like wildfire: only minutes ago I'd dropped the car at the garage. "Someone's playing funny buggers, hey?" The grin on Mr. Ledder's face seemed designed to make me uneasy. Mr. Stackhouse also appeared pleased with himself, but I stood straight, smiling back, and he started looking nervous. "Cameron," Mr. Ledder asked, "if you were to tamper with someone's car, so as to scare them, how would you do it?"

Mr. Stackhouse scratched his chin. "Maybe I'd take all the oil from the sump."

I giggled. "What's the sump?"

"Oh, well," he answered, "you'd have to get under the car and remove the oil by undoing the sump plug, or—" he coughed, watching as I smoothed my hair. "Or, I guess you'd put pinholes through the brake leads. Gradually, after about twenty minutes or so, all the brake fluid leaks out . . ."

"No," corrected Mr. Ledder. "The best way, I reckon, would be to remove the plug at the alternator. The battery would slowly lose charge, stalling. That's good because no warning light would spring up on the dashboard." He squinted at me. "You should've seen a warning light on the car's dash, last night."

I looked up at him through lowered lashes. "I didn't notice it."

Mr. Stackhouse continued thoughtfully, "You could loosen the petrol plug, but," he admitted, "you might smell petrol escaping."

"Mate, there's always sugar in the petrol tank." The two men started to laugh but when I joined in, they grew silent. Mr. Stackhouse explained the joke to me: "Sugar blocks up the carburetor. Everything. People use sand or sugar." He shook his head. "The bag of sugar in the petrol tank, or at least five hundred grams, and it runs up the pipes and into the carburetor and fuel injection system. Then you hear of divorcées, and that, bringing it in coughing and spluttering."

The men both stared at the ground.

Still smiling, I excused myself. Thomas was standing on the side of the oval, yelling to his son. "Watch the ball!" he bellowed. "Watch the damn ball!" Usually I saw him wearing business suits; now he was dressed in leisure wear that was fashionable ten years ago. A jacket with the wrong collar; jeans cut in the wrong style. The clothes weren't shabby. In fact, they looked expensive, premeditated. I sighed: no one— at least no one I knew—would wear aviator sunglasses like that, except as a joke. If I caught, say, my own father wearing those sunglasses, I'd shoot him down with machine-gun laughter. Now I didn't care. I just wanted to be alone with Thomas. I wanted him to take me back to the hotel, and this time I'd be better behaved. He was not someone who'd cope well with rejection. Some very intelligent people, if treated badly by their peers as adolescents, develop a kind of mega-lomania that, unfortunately, I seemed to find attractive. What if after Thomas had dropped me at school yesterday, he'd found my car, tampered with the brakes, and cut the fan belt as practice for my throat? I had tried to end our affair as we drove back from the hotel. He was telling me, "You can leave, but first you'll have to die."

A tiny rip developed in this sporting picture, and I sensed the menace underneath. The ball flew through the air like a scarlet bird. On the boys' white clothes, its stain was indeli-ble. The boys were so serious about this game, as serious as their fathers. "When my son puts his cricket whites on and pads up, he looks like an eighteen-year-old," I heard one father say. "Like a gladiator." The boys' poses were very mas-culine. The fielders swung their arms, practicing spin bowl-ing. They mimicked what they'd seen on television. One child spat vigorously every thirty seconds, slapping any skinny friend on the back. Another child caught the ball, and then dived down, rolling with it, his arms outstretched in vic-tory. *After this, nothing will ever seem so green.* One day these kids would realize this grass was the green of memory, but for now puberty seemed like a foreign disease they'd never have to catch.

The children's attention spans were not exhaustive, and before long their legs-apart, hands-on-hips poses became slightly louche. A fielder put an arm to waist, hips pivoted. Another draped a wrist casually over his head: a little dying slave. In the sun, their whites were as bright as pale marble. A butterfly fluttered over the pitch, a light spot on one's retina. To look at the boys I had to shield my eyes. They were statues on a well-kept lawn, in poses sketched by a noble to inspire other pedophiles. This was his garden of contemplation and each figure stood in silent dialogue. If children are born of original sin, Lucien's statue was helping the others to remain saturated in wickedness. Little did the adults know that this child, despite his lack of popularity, was leading the children's discussion on the merits of hell.

Billy: *How come if scientists say we were apes, Adam and Eve were human?*

Henry: *How do we know they weren't apes?*

Lucien: *Maybe apes evolved into Adam and Eve.*

Darren: *They wouldn't have had names; they'd just be Oooga and Booga.*

Billy: *How could Oooga and Booga know how to talk? Who recorded what they said?*

Alastair: *Snakes can't talk.*

Darren: *They might be able to.*

Lucien: *They can't speak* our *language. Their teeth are too small, and their tongues are too small to make the*

*right sounds. And it's virtually impossible for us to
teach a snake anything, because over the years their
instincts have taught them not to trust us.*

How would I tell Thomas that this affair had to end?
Would he grant me an exit pass for the sake of his son? "My
darling," I practiced. "I couldn't bear to be the cause of sadness. What if Lucien saw us together, and told his mother we
were hugging with no clothes on? Oh Lord! Then you'd
come home, and Lucien would ask, 'Daddy, what's a whore?
What is a slattern?' My heart would break if that happened,
for you and me, but mostly, for him . . ." I paused: this
approach would not necessarily work. If it were Veronica
who was the puppet master, I'd need to appeal to her directly.
And would the two of us really be able to strike a deal? The
rules of this game were complicated and ever changing. As
soon as I grew tired of playing, apparently, the consequences
would be dire.

Darren: *I think God is a phoney.*
Henry: *He'll kill you for saying that!*
Darren: *What does he do for us? He doesn't do anything
    for us.*
Alastair: *Like he doesn't give us gifts.*
Henry: *He doesn't send any of his helpers down.*
Billy: *Even if God was real, what does he do for us? So
    long ago were all the stories that no one believes
    anymore. Well, that's when they had angels and stuff,
    and now they don't have angels, so why's the point.
    Because why doesn't he send any angels down now?*

Alastair: *If Jesus is dead, why don't they send down Jesus's son?*
Lucien: *He didn't have a wife.*

Thomas was leaning over a children's water fountain. These fountains were designed for five-year-olds, they were built low, but he looked so graceful bending down to drink, so natural. Nearby a jacaranda tree was swaying, its purple flowers pimpish. He rose with water on his chin and I almost rushed to wipe it, but stopped myself. Up close he looked tired. When he saw my pretty dress, he did a double take. Smiling slowly he asked, "How are you?"

"I'm well. You?"

"Lucien isn't concentrating today." Thomas scratched his head. "The ball may as well be invisible."

"Has something upset him?"

Thomas raised an eyebrow. "Last night, after his mother returned from her reading, was tough, very tough."

"Oh dear. How is Veronica doing?"

"She's putting on a brave face."

"Gosh." I stood next to him, watching the play. "It was a bad night all round." I paused. "Someone messed with my car's brakes and cut the fan belt."

He looked unfazed. "It probably just snapped."

"And the brakes?" Something in my expression conveyed my suspicions.

"Oh, you don't think . . . ?" He laughed. "You don't think Veronica?" He laughed again.

"Of course not!" We stood next to each other, both staring straight ahead. "But have you ever . . ." I stuttered, "has it ever occurred to you that it was Graeme Harvey who killed Ellie?"

"Not you too!" Thomas erupted. "No, that's crazy." His brow furrowed. "He's guilty because you can't find his wife? He did it only because he seduced the girl, he bound her to him."

"How did he do that?"

"With his dick," Thomas muttered.

I tucked a lock of hair behind my ear. "Do you think, in any way, that months"—I paused—"years later, Graeme was relieved?"

"He loved that girl. Why would he be relieved?"

"Well," I answered coolly, "it tied up a loose end."

Thomas waited a moment. "No." He shook his head. "He thought she would marry and have children. That's not a loose end. He thought she would marry the most right of all the Mr. Wrongs: that is not a loose end." Thomas turned to me, and said in a soft sly voice, "He would think of her sometimes, and he'd smile at how he'd been one of her adventures. And he would remember how she'd walked; and how she'd sounded; and how, for him, she did her funny dance . . ."

Cicadas were chanting. The new day was electric. I wanted the fathers to stop watching us. They were congregated under the cypress tree, paying too close attention. They should've been watching the match. I pointed to the field, as if fascinated: on cue, Billy started to run but I didn't know why. I simply admired the anarchy of the boys' game. By next year their motor skills would be improved and much of this slapstick fun over. "Lucien just doesn't watch the ball," Thomas repeated.

"Could there be a problem with his sight?"

"No, he just doesn't concentrate."

"Maybe you're too competitive, Mr. Marne."

His face grew stern. "Are you being a good girl?"

"Yes." I pouted. "I'm being good." It was better for Thomas to think I still believed in him. "A very good girl." I gave a tiny moan. Confronted on that school excursion by my lover's wife—a woman who exuded so much sexual urbanity—I'd felt deeply competitive, a kind of fury. I'd realized I was backed into a corner with all my willed innocence. And afterward, trying to turn this to my advantage, I'd started talking to Thomas in a nuanced baby talk. It wasn't so much the manner of a child, as of a fourteen-year-old girl who was perhaps slightly simple.

"What did you do when you woke up?" he asked. "Did you eat your breakfast?"

"Yes, I was good."

"Did you wash your little face?"

I fidgeted with my skirt. "Yes."

"Did you do anything else?"

"No, I didn't." I bit my lip. "I wasn't. It wasn't me . . ."

"You brushed your teeth." Thomas waited. "And then you got all dressed up for the grown-ups. Did you want to make all the other kids' dads hot? Hmm? Did you want the other kids' dads to look at you?"

I bridled, throwing back my head. "Maybe."

"Tell me what you want them to do to you?"

"To give me toffees."

"Yes."

"And they could buy me sunglasses."

"And would you suck their cocks?"

"Would I get to keep the sunglasses?"

Stretching, I turned in time to see Veronica come strolling through the gates. She wore a sun hat and with her long white neck there was an orchid look about her, as if she were shrinking from the sun, but not too much.

Imagine if every time you walked into a room, people thought of murder. The fathers—and now some mothers— watched as Veronica walked toward us. It was the usual practice for the mothers to join their husbands with refreshments. They also brought along the little sisters and more family dogs. Gossiping and cheering everyone on, their presence made this whole scene less primordial, or maybe more so—I wasn't sure. How did the other mothers react to Veronica? *Murder at Black Swan Point* tended to be very popular with women of a certain age, just not in this neighborhood. They had all heard stories of Mrs. Marne driving down Murder Road to visit Ellie's parents: "Hello!" she'd apparently greeted the old woman who'd opened the door. "I'm Lisa. I was in your daughter's class at school." Mrs. Siddell had apologized for her poor memory, ushering the true-crime writer into a small, neat parlor. "Tell me about your school friends. Do you girls keep in touch?" "Some of us do." Veronica scoured her surroundings for any decorative flourish to spin through the story. As she noted the heavy drapes and wallpaper, now peeling, she took a photo of Lucien out of her wallet, and started talking of her own life, post high school.

"Listen," I whispered to Thomas, "I need to talk to you. I'm in trouble." My stare was intense. "Please."

"Today's a bad day," he said under his breath. "Today's a very bad day. Hello, darling!" he called.

Veronica wore a sheer silver blouse with a lace camisole

underneath. A gray crushed-silk skirt. Ballet slippers. It was like a fashion spread where the stylist chooses the most devastating suburban scene—a bowls club raffle; trash and treasure in the local church hall—then inserts the model. Veronica took off her hat. She kissed her husband, then turned to me, smiling. "Miss Byrne, how's everything going?"

"Very well, thank you."

"The class is okay?"

"Yeah, it's going fine, it's going really great." I paused. "Except for one thing."

The Marnes both turned.

"Yesterday afternoon someone cut my fan belt and loosened a brake caliper!"

Veronica looked horrified. "That's terrible. Have you reported it to the police?"

Thomas interjected, "The thing about fan belts is that they can snap." He crossed his arms. "Fan belts can snap, and you just can't really tell."

I stared at him. "What about the caliper?"

He sighed, shrugging. "Well, from what I understand, it was an old car." His face was stony. "It probably needed a service . . ."

"Could someone be trying to hurt Kate?" Veronica interrupted.

"It would be difficult to prove."

"Someone with a grudge?"

"The more I think of it," Thomas told her, "the more unlikely it sounds."

"I see." Veronica's expression softened, and she spoke slowly. "You're overwhelmed, Kate. It must be hard for you being so far away from your family."

I paused, slightly hypnotized. "Yes. It has been."

She gathered her mane of hair, pulling it over her shoulder. "Is this the first time you've lived away from home?" I nodded. "Well, I think you've been very brave coming and staying here all alone. Very brave." She looked at me closely. "You must feel vulnerable?"

"Sometimes."

"How old are you, Kate?"

"I'll be twenty-three next month."

"Well, you were right to move away," she said. "These feelings are natural." Thomas groaned quietly, but she ignored him, advising, "Now it's time to grow up."

I gasped for breath, coughing, and she patted my back. "It's all right. Let it out. Let it out." Before me the horizon line trembled: I'd been dumped by a wave. I stood feeling its slap, the way it belted my body. If you're unaccustomed to malice, it's shocking that someone would bear you ill intent. It's like receiving a dream kick or a dream bullet. You've been injured, but since there's no physical scar, one discounts the violence as imaginary. "Let it out." Veronica continued patting my back. She was privy to every intimacy. She had told me to grow up because she even knew of my baby talk.

I finished coughing, and Veronica waited for some response. "Thank you." Lightly touching her arm, I added, "I was speaking to my mother. And I just want you to know, she and her friends have been really moved by your book."

Veronica raised her hand to block sun from her brow. She looked grave. "That means so much." She closed her eyes. "The readers' support has just been totally overwhelming." She smiled a radiant smile, before reaching out to squeeze my hand. Then Veronica turned to her husband, and very naturally—the way one does when one's body is aligned closely to another's—he put his arm around her. I had heard it said, actually by Thomas, that in a threesome if one woman gets out of the bed to go and sit in a corner, rocking back and forward, shaking and crying to herself, it's not because of any noble reason; it's because the crying woman senses (correctly) that the other woman is preferred. I looked down at the ground. "Will you excuse me, Mrs. Marne, Mr. Marne."

I moved closer to the other parents. The Marnes were gaslighting me, slowly driving me crazy. As far as Veronica was concerned, Thomas was only sleeping with me to benefit her work. And perhaps she was right . . . I imagined her trying to write the most difficult part of *Murder at Black Swan Point*, trying to feel murderous: Enter Thomas, disheveled, wild-eyed, after an afternoon at my grandparents' house. He'd lean down to kiss her and she'd ask snakily, "Have fun?" She'd hand him a pencil, and he'd be about to draw diagrams, when she'd let fly with a tirade of abuse; the rudest, cruelest words. Then more calmly, in fact with the calm that only came with this inspiration, Veronica would have asked Thomas to leave, so she could complete the chapter. I had been the sacrificial lamb, a third party used to induce a jolt of frisson. They were the finest, the most refined criminals. It made sense—some jewel thieves orgasm during robberies.

I found myself laughing. Laughter which made people turn and stare. If Veronica had convinced Thomas to join her replaying the Black Swan Point story, perhaps she'd need to watch her own back. She must have known, in fact better than anyone, the tale's alternative ending. The police searched tire-

lessly for Margot Harvey for two weeks; then declared her
deceased. It was ruled that on the balance of evidence she had
contributed to Eleanor Siddell's killing. But what had happened to her? Why was Margot's blood found all over her
house? Presumably Veronica had tried to find the answer.

The locals claimed she'd visited Graeme Harvey in the
cancer ward, bearing an opulent bouquet. She had also taken
along some crime photos hoping to jog his memory. It was
suspicious that Margot had left so few traces at the crime
scene. It was suspicious that the abandoned station wagon
was spotless. However, what really confused Veronica was
why it took the pathologist's testimony to jolt the good vet
from his concussion? In the ward, Mrs. Marne had reached
into her briefcase and pulled out the photos. She felt the
poignancy of this exchange. She was helping him confront
his ghosts: "Here's your blood on the blue shag bath mat.
Here's your wife's blood too. How did she come to bleed
again? You do remember, don't you?" The dying man tried to
scream but without his trachea made very little noise. A
nurse checking the room, saw Veronica on the verge of tears.
"Oh! A visitor: lovely! I'll leave you a bit longer."

The boys' cricket whites billowed against their skinny bodies;
the material, on their backs, like sails. It was strange, but
despite the Marnes' threats for the first time in a long while
I felt totally alive. I felt as if every particle was swimming
before me with improved resolution. Fear, like guilt, must
have a way of increasing the pixelation of everyday life. It was
Lucien's turn to bat. He walked onto the oval, staring down

as if wishing to be swallowed. I shook my head. The relationship between teacher and student was so intimate. People gave me their children every morning. I had them for the whole day. Then, these same people gave me the children again the next morning. For eight months the kids had been like members of my family. I taught them their most essential lessons: how to read, how to write, how to treat others. I taught them skills they'd have for the rest of their lives.

Lucien got into position, holding the bat the way his father had shown him. He was trying hard to concentrate, but looked panicked. Thomas stood nearby yelling directions. Watching his child, it was easier to understand him: he had probably been hardened day by day.

The bowler took a long run, and it seemed forever until he threw the ball. It missed the wicket, and an ancient dog with a windup tail snatched it in his mouth, then hobbled away. A chase ensued: the dog was apprehended, but refused to drop it. "*Drop the ball!*" "*Drop! Drop!*" The bored fielders were having a hard time standing still. While a father negotiated with the dog, the fielders were air-batting, or air-bowling, or fiddling with themselves.

Lucien was trembling with concentration. His father called out, and the boy smiled weakly in his direction. Another ball flew toward him: he missed it. An expression came over Lucien's face I hadn't seen before. He looked frightened. His father called again, angrily. The boy looked toward Thomas as the ball approached, and it shot past him for the third time.

How many parents will admit their fantasy is to be childless? I watched Lucien fight back tears. His body language revealed his fit in the world; his shoulders were stooped, his gaze averted. For a long time I'd thought it the pose of a young philosopher. It was also the pose of a child not wanting to be seen. The Marnes had fostered their son's mature demeanor because they couldn't stand the "kidness" of him. Thomas had written me his long notes about curricula so he didn't have to talk to Lucien about hopscotch and the tooth fairy. The tragedy of parenthood must be that you make this baby, and you start off loving the baby in all the ways you wanted to be loved. Then the baby, slowly, grows into something you don't recognize: a separate person with your own worst faults. The tragedy of having children must be learning firsthand that in every parent there's a black box of infanticidal thoughts. Lucien had drawn pictures of himself blind, beheaded, and bullet-ridden: who would be most likely, in his wildest nightmares, to perform such atrocities? According to child psychologists, often monsters are mothers and fathers in disguise.

The batting team was reacting to Lucien's poor play in high-drama mode. They were shaking their heads, kicking at the grass. The fielders were playing air guitar and sitting down in mock contemplation, staring at the sky. Thomas seemed just as revolted by his son's form. Darren called out, expressing Mr. Marne's opinion: "You play like a girl!" Even the kids on Lucien's team laughed and sniggered. "Lucy! Lucy!" they started yelling and their parents did nothing to stop them.

Lucien stood holding the bat. For a split second it seemed the tears would spill. Then he smiled good-naturedly. He smiled at full volume. And I remembered the textbook had suggested that if a young child spontaneously added to his drawing a unicorn, or butterflies, or a rainbow, one was supposed to heed the warning. Aren't they meant to draw these things, one might have thought; didn't I? Apparently in stressful situations young children will draw what appears to be happy: just as we think we should pretty up the truth for them, they do it straight back.

"Lucy!" the boys called, then they clapped. "Lucy!" Clap-clap-clap. "Lucy!"

Lucien smiled merrily, like he was in on the joke. He was smiling even as he was bowled out. The bails flew off, and the winning team tried to make that primordial noise, that tribal noise to do with winning that comes from deep within one's belly: a guttural roar like the cricket spectators made on television. Their voices had not yet broken, however, so the noise was high and choirboy sweet. The boys threw their hands in the air, all yelping with delight. From a distance they looked like gulls. They ran to each other, slapping their friends on their backs. In the melee, Lucien tossed his white hat over his head. The hat blew a few feet away, and while the others were hugging, he ran to catch it. He threw it again and again, and the same absurd thing kept happening. Thomas's face was blank with humiliation. But I understood what Lucien was doing. He was adding butterflies, and unicorns, and a rainbow. And take note, I thought, by being so merry he was sabotaging his enemies' plans.

I smoothed my dress over my hips and smiled. An icecream van, with cones painted naively on the paneling, pulled up in all its psycho-clown glory. The children on the field—especially those from the losing team, crying—now perked up. They forgot about the cricket, consumed by the age-old dilemma: "Should I get a rocket ice cream with competition details inside, or a spaceman with a bubblegum nose?" All the boys were filthy with grass stains, trying to do deals. Negotiations had begun regarding sleepovers or play dates for the evening. Younger kids ran around catching insects in their drink bottles. Some first-graders were scaling the walls of the girls' toilet block. This was Oedipal athletics: if the little gender warriors saw the secret way girls tinkled they'd all rule the world, or spin into a decline.

I stood near some mothers, wanting to blend in. They talked in hushed tones without acknowledging me. Surely they'd heard, like their husbands, what had happened to my car. Everyone must have known. They all ignored me, peevish about some lesson I'd taught they'd found offensive. Trying to stay calm, I approached Lillian Hurnell. She was holding her two small dogs on a lead, talking closely to Dawn Nesbit, the physical education teacher. "Isn't it a stunning day?" I called.

"It's still quite chilly, Kate," Lillian answered. "If you've got a fever, perhaps you should wear a cardigan."

"I think I got excited to see summer coming."

"Perhaps a bit too excited," said Dawn.

I glared. Dawn, with her lace ankle socks and cutoff overalls, was not very good with other women. I noticed, however, how quick she was to console any fathers in need. Every time she complimented a boy on his batting or hand-eye coordination, it was really a way of complimenting the father. These men looked at Dawn all the more closely, thinking, I guess she's not *that* ugly. It was an ingenious way of luring them into her web. I wondered how many she had slept with—she'd been teaching here an awfully long time.

"The Marnes should've put that boy in the car," Dawn said, "and driven him straight home." She and Lillian turned to stare at the couple. While Lucien purchased an ice cream, Veronica stood waiting, looking uncomfortable. Thomas was drowning his sorrows with a beer.

"Can't children be mean?" I thought aloud. "So breathtakingly mean to each other? At least adults have codes." My voice sounded strange. "But a child will say: 'I hate you!'; 'All the kids hate you!'; 'You are ugly, you smell.'" I laughed. "'All the freckles on your face look like flecks of shit!'"

"Kate," Lillian interrupted. "Will you be the garbage monitor, please?"

Dawn grinned: this was usually a job for two fourth-graders.

"Of course, Lillian." I went to get the bin and the kids came up, dropping their rubbish inside. Soon it was heavy with soda cans and rejected sandwiches. I could barely drag it.

"Let me help you!" Nursing his beer, Thomas strolled over. Everyone stopped talking. Even the children waiting for their ice creams turned to watch. He took one handle, and together we started carrying the bin to the recycling station behind the art room. Thomas, unaffected by the attention, stared hungrily at my floral dress. Like a villain in a silent movie, all his carnality registered in his eyes and eyebrows. I gazed past him, back to the wall of staring faces. No longer was there such a thing as safety. No longer was there right or wrong. Now everyone seemed to me as though they were descended from a convict. The butcher had been sent down *for enticing a young female into his hut, giving her cakes, and taking liberties with her.* The baker had been *singing an indecent song.* The rich man: *whilst at Impression Bay he made cards from the leaves of the Bible,* and was given thirty lashes. The poor man: he *attempted against the order of nature to commit with a ewe the detestable and abominable crime called buggery.*

Behind the art room wall, out of view, I dropped the bin. "How long has Veronica known for?"

He took a deep breath. "Since, I don't know, the beginning."

"Why didn't you tell me?"

"Why did you presume I wouldn't tell her?" He stared into the rubbish bin, then laughed. "She's probably relieved you take me off her hands. It's one less thing for her to worry about." He relaxed his face, straightened up, and looked at me with an expression I had never seen before; his features were so regular that he was blindingly handsome and completely inscrutable. "Would you like a drink?" He held out the beer bottle.

"You were talking about leaving her."

He sighed, and then in his lawyer-voice, told me, "Kate, marriage is a complicated thing. It's very hard for two intelligent . . ." He paused, a smile forming. "Marriage is complicated." He had started to unbutton my dress, and he could now see clearly I wasn't wearing a bra. Leaning down, he pinned me against the wall. At first I tried to struggle, but he was forceful, and receiving his kisses I remembered again why people kiss. I wanted to put my lips to his face and take the tiredness from it. I wanted to show him I could make him lighter. The ice-cream van sang a tinny carnival song. I received each kiss, scared the whole blue recycling bin would tip over and spill, too electrified to move. When finally I did pull away I reached for the beer bottle and took a swig. "It tastes funny. Drinking it makes me feel funny."

He ran his fingers through his hair. "Where does it make you feel funny?"

"I don't like to say."

"Tell me then"—he raised my skirt—"what you learned today at school."

I jutted my chin. "Today's Saturday."

"Tell me what you learned last week."

I twisted a lock of hair as he slid his hand between my legs. "*James and the Giant Peach* is a book by Roald Dahl about a boy who likes sex." Wide-eyed, I whispered, "This boy likes entering the peach. It's warm and sweet."

Thomas ran his index finger along the line of my breast. "Your skin is glowing."

"Oh, I was playing in the playground." I moaned. "I like the swing and the slide."

"The monkey bars?" He smiled.

"Yes, I like that." His finger was now inside me.

"No one saw your underpants did they?"

"I don't think so."

"What noise does the kitty-cat make?"

"*Meow.*"

"What noise does the horsey make?"

I trembled. "*Neigh.*"

"And when he swishes his tail?"

"Oh, *Swish-swish.*"

"You're a smart little girl."

"I like animals," I said breathlessly. "I once found a baby bird, oh, and fed him honey."

"Does this hurt?"

"Oh no." I leaned against him. "The big boys do this all

the time." I moaned again. "Should I be talking to you? I'm not supposed to . . ."

We heard footsteps. Quickly I broke away, scrambling to pull up my underwear. I wagged my finger at Thomas, but his face was tired, and he only shook his head. Just as he stepped back from our embrace, just as I buttoned up my dress, Lucien came behind the shed, carrying a Space Invader ice cream. Lucien, with his father's eyes and eyelashes and half-smile, looked first at Thomas, then at me, and back to Thomas again. The garbage smell made me feel ill.

"Lucien, you're not supposed to eat those!" The ice cream had a bubblegum nose.

"Dad, I'm not going to swallow it."

"It's not good for you."

"I'm not a baby!"

"Lucien, give it to me!"

Thomas took the ice cream from his son. He dug out the bubblegum nose with his wet index finger. Rolling the gumball, blue food dye stained his skin. I watched him realize that he couldn't throw the gum in the trash, while this little boy stood watching; all the hat-throwing bravado stripped away.

"You bowled very well today, Lucien," I said quickly.

Lucien just stared at his noseless spaceman, making a grunt.

"Thanks for your help, Mr. Marne."

I walked away, sad for Lucien: I could hear Thomas engaging him in a conversation about his cricket form. Now his bowling had improved, his batting needed some extra attention. I reported back to Lillian Hurnell, who was standing with a group of parents. My walk may have been jaunty, full of rude intonations, because when I asked, "Is there anything else I can do?" Lillian stared at me, then at my dress, without smiling. "Why don't you go home, Kate? You've done quite enough today."

I looked down and noticed two buttons were still undone from our embrace. "Well, I guess I'll see you Monday."

She didn't answer.

I walked out the gates, and felt a wave of disapproval rising within me: *Imagine fucking your own child's teacher!* How could he do that? Even if the boy was a poor sportsman, how could he do that? *It was disgusting!* She was a young woman, a barely hatched woman, away from home for the first time. A little naive, I smiled. A little out of her depth. At the very beginning of a career to which she was possibly ill suited. Living in a shit-hole town when she could have been doing a masters in child psychology or any-other-fucking thing!

As I made my way down the Main Street I had to pass the silver car. Thomas seemed cross, and Veronica looked over, barely managing the mask of politeness she usually had perfected. Thomas was trying to persuade Lucien to take his grass-stained shoes off before getting into the backseat; the cramped backseat of his expensive car that I knew all too well. He was taking off his shoes the same slow, cross-legged way as my old lover. "Lucien, hurry up, will you?" Thomas said impatiently. He wasn't being cruel; he was just being a father. Still, it was unattractive to watch. I'd quite liked it when Thomas disciplined me, but it was almost sickening that he did it to someone else—and so seriously. I suddenly wished Lucien and I could just leave and go somewhere safe together, away from these people.

Improvising with great aplomb.

*T*ry *it again, Kitty!"*

Using an old beer bottle, the bushland creatures replayed a key scene. Percy Possum, Kitty's acting partner, wrapped himself around a silver gum branch, getting into character. Percy was a renowned gossip, having lived in nearly all the locals' roofs, but his dramatic flair made for an invigorating performance. Percy raised a paw to his brow. "Yes! Yes! I have betrayed all our vows," cried the possum, giving the rendition his all. "I am an adulterer!"

Oh! The animals winced as Kitty picked up the bottle. Improvising with aplomb, the koala opened her vacant eyes wide. She brought great insight to Margot's plight, capturing her rage and humiliation and—after miming the bottle strike— her horror at having bloodied her beloved husband. As the two performers took their bows, the assembled animals offered polite congratulations. But they were all thinking the same thing: why had Graeme Harvey not alerted the police to the mixed blood- stains on his bedroom and bathroom floors? He must have real- ized they did not belong solely to him—his wife's blood had also been spilled.

"Being the victim of a crime's fallout can be extremely upset- ting, even leading to what's known as post-traumatic stress dis- order," Terence Tiger now advised his friends. "Memories can become vague and disorganized; apparent falsehoods may be the result of nervous shock rather than any deliberate attempt to mislead."

"So Dr. Harvey may have just been a little forgetful?" inquired Kitty Koala hopefully.

"Balderdash!" Wally Wombat growled. "If he had post- traumatic stress disorder, we all do!"

The animals looked at one another. Unfortunately, the years since Ellie's death had not been kind to any of them. They'd trav- eled around this fair isle solving human crimes, while so many of their furry brethren, their feathered cousins, and most reptil- ian relatives had had foul and bloody deeds committed against them. Wally's family had had dreadful luck with feral cats and cars. *Kingsley Kookaburra flew around and around, suffering some Lear-like delirium. That drunken wallaby, Warwick, had been shot through the eyes: for knowing too much, or for pet food. And poor Kitty, they never mentioned it, but like many of her species, she had a strain of chlamydia that had led to blindness and infertility . . . she was unable to have any little bears.*

Still, it was better to look on the bright side.

"That's a bit grim, Wally," Terence Tiger said finally. "Frightfully grim, actually." Waiting a moment for the tension to pass, the tiger cleared his throat and announced, "Chums! I've something else to show you." With a flourish he pulled out a set of drawings, by Lucien Marne, after actual crime photographs. The bushland gang all gasped. How did the tiger always manage to sniff out such evidence? "It's a funny thing," Terence said in his dry way, "but when you're extinct, people look you straight in the eye and assume they haven't seen you."

All the animals, including the wombat, laughed knowingly. They studied the crayon drawings of Graeme Harvey's wounded head, while listening to Terence. "Lucien's fine sketches illustrate one of the case's central dilemmas. The bottle, with which Margot was supposed to have hit her husband, never turned up. The police asked Graeme repeatedly if he had any idea how it might have been disposed of. No. The crime squad searched extensively. No success." The tiger sighed. "Some people began to wonder if Graeme's whole story about Margot attacking him was apocryphal. Could he have acquired those cuts in another altercation? Was there something he was hiding?"

The animals turned, as if from the conversation, and through some shrubbery saw Miss Kate Byrne, walking down the Main Street. A wide-eyed young bear described to Kitty what the schoolteacher was wearing. "I'm glad she chose that floral dress," said the older koala in her maternal way. But secretly, she felt worried. "Was the lass really so foolish?" Kitty stifled a groan. "Oh no! Did she actually believe that cracking the Siddell case would put her out of danger?"

THE PUB'S WALLS, stained nicotine yellow, displayed a variety of mounted sharks' jaws and the memorabilia of long-wrecked whaling ships. The whalers once sat in here waiting for the whales to spout, but if the seas were rough, they'd stay drinking for days. Now a row of old men clung to one side of the bar, as if, for them, the seas had been too rough for years. I sat opposite. Perhaps I had intuitively positioned myself next to the men's toilets, although I preferred to think this was my default position: the teacher surveying her class. Men played darts. Men watched the flickering horses. Men smoked. Signals were rising from each mute drunk. I had expected to be leered at, but what I read was resentment. My presence interrupted their secret business. They could try to pretend they were alone, until nature called, then each man swung past me, indignant still, as he held himself close. Some of the fathers were amongst the drinkers. If they approached, I knew I'd breathe fire. A line had been crossed. Every molecule was now changing, and the knife was in my purse.

"How's your day been, love?" the barmaid asked. She was a plump redhead, sunburned on the back of her neck. No one in the pub had to order his beer. The barmaid just looked out the window, saw a patron's truck approaching, and pulled him a glass.

"My day's been great."

"Take it easy?"

"Yes, yes, nice and easy."

She walked away and I stared back into my drink. Unfortunately, *Murder at Black Swan Point* would offer no clues as to the Marnes' plans. Each chapter ended with another unanswered question, right until the book's end where Veronica, trying to be poignant, wrote of visiting Point Puer's convict ruins, in search of Margot's fate. Walking to the edge of the Suicide Cliffs, Veronica had thrown flowers into the sea, mourning a brave woman who'd been undone by her passion. "Perhaps within all of us," Veronica confessed, "there is an island of the night, and on that island a castaway capable of deeds we'd rather not acknowledge." Veronica's castaway was certainly capable of being verbose. The truth of this finale was that its author had no idea what had happened— 315 pages, but all she'd needed to scratch on each was I DON'T KNOW.

I put my head in my hands. The Marnes' collusion made me feel an old angry feeling. My imagination had hit a wall and, swerving down a dark corridor, I started thinking of my own parents. I started thinking of my mother and father standing in for the Harveys rather than Veronica and Thomas. Graeme Harvey was roughly my father's age. A strange, stiff-upper-lip generation to be born into, because although everyone liked to regard Tasmania as an outpost of Britain—singing "God Save the King," then the Queen, around the flag at school assemblies—they had to live with history in a way most people who consider themselves civilized do not. My father went to the same boys' school as Dr. Harvey, but was three grades below him. This school was built on a graveyard. To construct the Junior Wing the ground had to be leveled. Bones poked out of the earth, and it was realized some of the coffins would need to be exhumed. When the chains of a crane accidentally broke, a coffin came crashing down into the school's playground. One little boy was expelled for running up and trying to prod a wedding ring off a skeleton's finger.

The stories of the teachers' brutality have always seemed like cartoon episodes. There was the black-eyed master from Wales who'd beaten the little boys with "daps," or running shoes. One day, when someone had been bad, the man asked for a "dap." Several of the boys ran out to get one, and were then beaten too, for not having asked to be excused. There was the little boy sent to the headmaster to show him Good Work. The headmaster turned apologetically to the mother, with whom he was taking tea, claiming, "I shan't be long!" as he proceeded to give the child a quick caning. It was hard to believe that these children were my father and my father's friends, that they were ever excited about losing their baby teeth, that their faces once trembled into bouts of tears.

I surveyed the men around me. I imagined them learning to read, one word at a time, their index fingers leading them through an odyssey with shipwrecks and poisonous snakes: *A Boy's Adventures in the Wilds of Australia; Roughing It in Van Diemen's Land; The Castaways of Disappointment Island.* Learning to read just after the war, they probably had slightly older books, stories about an Antipodean Wild West with bushfires and escaped convicts exacting revenge. Hook-Handed Bill ripped up his victims with his hook. Boys with bows and arrows hunted emu. "With some difficulty, for the wood was still pretty wet, I got a fire kindled and roasted a parrot." In the illustrations, stained brown with foxing, the kangaroos didn't even look like kangaroos, they looked like horses with coarse, doggy fur. The Aborigines looked like American Indians, wearing togas, and red feathers in their hair.

There were probably old photos of these drunks in cricket teams together. There were photos of my father and his friends; black-and-whites from the early 1950s. It was amazing to me that the children in these prints looked just the same as the nine-year-olds at Endport Primary; they seemed, in some way, more like a different race than a different generation. They were guys who hung around saying dumb things; you had to laugh at their jokes for the appropriate amount of time, before asking to be excused. One of my father's friends, a surgeon, designed a dream house for himself and his wife but wouldn't even let her contribute to the layout of the kitchen. Another invited all his mates around the day his wife graduated from university. They took her desk and all her papers into the garden and lit a bonfire.

During the day Graeme Harvey got by, running on a feeling that he was outside himself. On farms that were really junkyards he couldn't stop his own theater. It was disgusting he cared what these men with burned-out faces thought of him. *I stay because my life is here.* He would get out of his car, and compose his face in warning: *My daughters love this place. It's their home. Should I have to leave my home? I can look people in the eye.* The farmers led him past their houses. Inside their wives hated him but made casseroles for his daughters. He and the farmers walked past fences that were really just a few slats that happened to be swaying together, giant gray driftwood waves about to break. *I stay because it's too hard at the moment.*

On the worst nights, Graeme Harvey lay in bed wondering if he had made some dare-wish to God, asking to be a single man. Had he killed the girl, then forgotten? He could picture himself prowling around outside her dark house, finding the open back door, walking in. She would have been fast asleep, her head stocked with girlish notions—Ellie hadn't realized that he'd have next to nothing if Margot divorced him. Margot held the purse strings. Her family owned their house. And Ellie? Graeme pictured her lying there. She had wanted so many things. All the things a girl from her lovely background thinks she deserves.

Old windows and doors leaned against the farm's aluminum shed; so did reels of rusted chicken wire. The animals inside seemed incidental; what was really being farmed were broken-down motors, pieces of engine grazing in the afternoon sun. *I stay because there's nowhere else I know. If I pack my bags I'm not sure where I'd head.* In the shed it stank of lanolin and excrement. He'd squat and listen to the animal's quickening heartbeat. If the farmer looked at him a certain way he thought of the girl with her throat cut. He thought of the time between the first stab and her losing consciousness. If the animal were dying he'd give it a shot quickly. Then something unspoken would pass between him and the other man. "I'm not thinking anything," the farmer may as well have said.

On the way back to the car, in the twilight, Dr. Harvey would see the sunset reflected in the dirty windows of the farmer's house. All purple and orange, there was a riot in the clouds. And superimposed, his own tired face. He took the casserole gratefully, leaving just in time: just before the weariness could no longer be modulated. He'd leave before he realized the stealing around before was just training for this new life of always walking into a room to win somebody back.

The barmaid refilled my glass, and I thought of my mother. I thought of my mother and the women, like Margot Harvey, whose desks were burned. They finished school and went to London on the boat. The world was their oyster for two years while they did temp jobs and took little trips. They lived in flats with other girls from school and were courted by the boys from home. At parties, men still stood on one side of the room by the beer keg, women on the other. It was the swinging sixties—the medical students had told their friends if you slept with a girl a week before, or a week after, her period, everything would be fine. Some men had bets they could crack girls; those who were good only had intercourse if it seemed an engagement was within sight. Girls were looking for husbands who were in the top half of the bell curve in terms of intelligence and had pleasant personalities, nice manners. The boys acted much as they had at home: drinking a lot, and smashing cars. All their lives were bound up in Australia. They all knew they'd go back and carry on as before, and when they settled down it would be forever.

Margot Harvey probably had other friends who returned home to find Life did not fit their plans. Their big adventure over, they settled down to the business of marriage and children. Then, just when they'd well and truly signed on the dotted line, the rules changed. All the things they'd expected, all the lessons they'd been taught, now counted for nothing. One woman my family knew had worked to put her husband through medical school: he ran off with his nurse. Another woman left her husband as she said she couldn't stand him anymore. The social revolution hit Australia ten years late, and people now supposedly divorced without stigma. But Margot Harvey had watched how divorce had wrecked her own mother. Margot had done everything right, every good-girl trick to avoid the same fate. When she realized it hadn't worked, she must have felt the old anger, starting like a wave, from far away and long ago, suddenly breaking inside her. And even then, after she had killed her husband's lover, it seemed this woman still returned to check whether, with Ellie dead, she could claim back her old life.

Turning her key in the lock, Margot walked inside and found her house looked just the same. The half-cooked dinner was on the stove and the smashed bottle lay on the floor. Margot took the dustpan from under the sink. She kneeled and filled the pan with shards and grit. Looking for splinters, her head close to the ground, she laid her forehead down. For a moment she stayed on the floor, almost in a ball. *I did this for you. I did this for our family.* When she got up she wrapped the glass in newspaper, and put the bundle in her coat pocket. She didn't want Graeme to wake and see the mess.

Margot walked down the hall to check on her daughters. Their naughty little girl bodies were splayed in strange poses. They'd had to wriggle into sleep. Toys were all over the floor and someone could have tripped. She felt the weight of the knife although her hand was empty. Sleeping, her daughters looked as they would when they were very old, spittle around their mouths, thin hair over tired faces.

Only hours ago she'd stood by the stove trying to make them dinner. She'd heard screaming: in the living room they were huddled in a corner while a bird, lost in the air, flapped its wings wildly. The bird kept stunning itself against a window. There'd be the dull thud as it hit the glass, then the girls' shrieks as they channeled each hopeless blow. Margot opened the glass doors. Cool air came into the room and the bird could've flown out. The bird could've walked out if it didn't want to fly. They willed it to leave like a guest no longer enjoying their company. It flew onto the couch as if settling in. Furious, Margot shooed the bird, and it tottered off on its little legs, not looking back at any of them. She had returned to the kitchen where again she heard the girls squealing. They'd found little pellets of shit everywhere. They now ran around finding the shit with glee. And in all this giggling and pointing they were living out some toilet joke. And this little, stubborn, unwanted bird was complicit in the laughing against her: Margot wanted to slap each of them. She wanted to give them each a good hiding. Instead she'd sent the girls to their rooms, turning off each pot boiling on the stove.

Across the hallway her husband was sleeping. He used to tell her every day she was the girl for him. At a restaurant he'd hold her hand under the table. He'd read to her the dishes on the menu. Asleep, he too looked older. He was curled up, his mouth wide open. It was the pose she'd seen in a magazine of a man found in peat; one of those people who stay not quite dead. When Graeme moaned she knew who was visiting his dream. She'd done the right thing. It was supposed to be the adulteress doomed to fall, but nowadays this girl could have gotten his love and his children and it would have been Margot as the divorcée wearing the badge of shame. Graeme's mouth was wide open like he'd been stunned. "Good." She walked into the bathroom and closed the door. His blood was still on the floor. "Good." She turned on the tap. She pulled up her sleeve and unpeeled the hand towel. Ellie had scratched at her wrist, breaking through the skin. Margot had had to turn on the overhead light in the girl's room; find a towel and then make a bandage. In Ellie's room of pretty things, she'd stopped her own bleeding, before taking a blanket from the twin bed to cover up the body.

Margot now looked down at the bathroom floor and realized she was bleeding. She put her hands in the basin, watching the water change color. She didn't want to see herself in the mirror. Already she would look like a ghost, pale and bloated, because the girl had blocked the sun. It made her start to cry. There was no point patching up the wound the way she'd learned at nineteen years old. There was no point.

She was going to have to leave her family again tonight and drive away forever.

I looked outside. In the golden hour, certain leaves had found their calling; a brick wall was illuminated like a sacred text. They say an answer is where the mind comes to rest. Without any explanation, all the possibilities branched off endlessly, each one ridden through with doom. Margot hadn't left behind a suicide note; she'd left nothing. This seemed strange: our desire to "not get lost," to leave a clue, is so strong. I had seen a small prayer book at Port Arthur. *Robert Maxwell is my name* was written carefully on the first page; *Robert Maxwell is my name* was written on every single page thereafter. People spoke so confidently of Margot having survived. Did she have a chartered boat waiting at the bottom of the Suicide Cliffs? Was there a lover at the helm? Did this couple sail away together?

The hours between Ellie Siddell's death and Margot Harvey's disappearance were easily the most intriguing part of the Black Swan Point story. It was possible Margot Harvey came home, wounded, after killing the girl and that that was when she left traces of blood on her bathroom floor. But if you imagine Margot leaving her family and running away to sea, the story quickly descends into cliché. People had never managed to reconcile the rumor that Margot survived with the rumor that Graeme was Ellie's murderer. If Graeme were the murderer, why would *Margot* have disappeared? The two stories were incompatible, but perhaps each one had an element of truth. Margot had not committed suicide, but then she'd also not run away. Graeme hadn't murdered Ellie, but he was a murderer: he had killed his wife after realizing what she had done.

Graeme Harvey hadn't had a dream for ten years, probably more. Not one damn dream for ten years; then, after Margot disappeared, often, he would fall asleep and she would visit him. He would dream that in the middle of that last night he had woken, hearing noise in the bathroom: Margot was shivering, washing her hands in the basin. Turning, she looked at him with the expression of a crazy person. She was pleased, proud, even, that she'd ruined his life. Suddenly she lurched forward, angry, trying to scratch out his eyes. She was scratching and clawing at his face. He stood still while she scratched him and then she told him what she'd done. Graeme couldn't help it. He put his hands around her neck. Tighter, then tighter again—she'd looked so pleased with herself.

Even in the dream his own calm surprised him. His wife's body felt heavy as he carried her to the car. One arm under her neck, the other under her knees: he was carrying her back over the threshold because things hadn't quite worked out. He was holding her closer than he had in a long time, still not believing she was dead. He laid her down in the backseat. The broken bottle, wrapped in newspaper, was in her coat pocket. As he drove to the cliff, he kept expecting she'd wake up and scream at him. He even thought this as he carried her to the edge. Afterward, he turned immediately and walked back up the track, past the car. He left the door unlocked with her handbag on the passenger seat. Walking home, he tried to think of nothing. He walked along the back roads. At dawn, the trees would keep their mouths shut; each leaf turning its blind eye.

From out of nowhere a car approached. It slowed and the driver wound down the window. It was an old friend. Someone they'd known in London and hadn't seen in years. Graeme was delighted. The friend asked after Margot. He asked after the children, then drove away. Graeme started sweating. No one ever used this road, but now there was another car. He kept walking. The car rolled up to him. "Would you like a lift?" It was another old friend. They smiled at each other, but then Graeme remembered why he was walking. "No. Thank you." The man drove away. Graeme was sweating, trying to get home. It seemed everyone now used this road. He was offered more rides, until finally he reached his house, exhausted, and crawled into bed. Just as he lay down, the dream became worse: Margot would always come out of the bathroom. With her clean hands she'd pull back the blanket to get into bed beside him. Suddenly he would remember a time when she made him smile with everything she did. He would feel a rush of love for her: his young wife—she had come home. She had come back to him.

Now I wavered on the bar stool, confused. The Harveys were unmasked and I had just imagined my parents killing me. First the murderer had been my father, then my mother. "This is disgusting!" Thomas and Veronica were my enemies.

And they were doing this, making me think these things, to make me insecure. I didn't know whether to laugh or cry. The Marnes had put ideas into my head, to make me doubt the one thing in which I could believe: "My parents love me!" I tried to sit still, but the drunkenness was in my spine; the lowest vertebrae were the worst affected. The room sounded of thudding hooves and the commentator's steady hum. My makeup felt stale; my hair stringy. This experiment—of being a woman—had failed; I had the sense I'd dressed up for a party to which no one was coming.

Once Thomas looked at me, and said, "You have a face that is terrific, and plain, and ugly all at once." I wished it would settle into being just terrific: beauty seemed an insurance policy you only paid for much later. People with plain faces aren't meant for interesting lives. If fate is a hunter you can't be the lion cub and jump up singing, "Take me!" Fate has to want you. A quiet truth floated before me: there's a psychosis unleashed by the fear of a boring life. Then, aloud, I thought, "No, that's wrong." I remembered driving around curve after curve being unable to stop. The Marnes wanted me gone, but there was no point guessing their next move. Each time I imagined the story's true ending, I was confronted by the same stark fact—the girl dies whichever way you play it. Knowing who the murderer had been wouldn't keep me safe.

Groaning, I thought of my parents alone in that house: my mother would come back from the supermarket and find my father up a ladder sweeping leaves from the guttering. She'd find him doing the things that should've been done years ago. She'd sit down and suddenly, from outside, hear the grunt as he raised his ax, and then the wood's inconsolable cry. He only wants to keep his baby warm, she'd think. He's the daddy. He has the whole world in his hands, and every time the ax strikes the wood he says a prayer she will be safe. She might get cold, he'd worry. He'd raise the ax and strike. This wood is good burning wood. Hard wood burns hotter and longer than soft wood, does she know that? He tried to remember if he'd explained that you get a better flame if it's a smaller piece . . .

"What if, after you died," I imagined Thomas asking, "your parents got a foster daughter?"

I glared, lowering my glass. Sometimes, by mistake, my father would call this girl Kate. She'd move into my bedroom, which my mother had been keeping as a sort of a shrine. Little by little, things would change. The walls of my room would be repainted; my clothes given to charity. Before long, all the neighbors would realize my parents were fully recovered. This new, improved family would have a garage sale, dispensing with boxes of my knickknacks. And that's when I'd become a ghost and haunt the living-fuck out of all of them! I raised my beer glass into the air. First someone had to do the killing: *Come and get me! I'm right here!* The glass trembled slightly as I swallowed. *Take a knife from your kitchen; take scissors from your sewing basket: all you women with your fallen bodies. In certain lights I look as unblemished as a twelve-year-old.* Through my drink the world was golden. *Come and get me, all you men with your fat guts, with your long-armed monkey walks. Open the bonnet and cut my fan belt clean in two!* I slammed the glass down on the bar. *I am still young! I am still young!*

SUDDENLY, AT THE next bar stool, perched Malcolm, the guide from the penal settlement. He asked if he could buy me a drink, and I sat smiling at him stupidly. "Sure." The barmaid had just refilled my glass. "I'd love a drink." He was oddly handsome, baby-faced, with whisker-free skin. He used props to gain gravitas: a cigarette hung from his plump lips; the sleeves of his purple cowboy shirt were rolled up, and his soft arms bore pen markings or practice tattoos. One arm said *Pow!* like a cartoon speech bubble. On the other was scrawled *Bad Fun*. Malcolm was nervous. You can tell when a man is attracted to you. His fingers, tapping against the bar, were long and delicate. You can just tell.

"I'd like a martini," I told the barmaid confidently.

She looked blank. "What do you want in it?"

I hesitated. "The usual things."

"What are they?"

"If the lady wants a martini," Malcolm said, all chivalry, "she should have it."

"Geoff, how do you make a martini?" the barmaid asked the drunkest of the drunks. He and the others all claimed to know, but she walked into the backroom swearing. Malcolm and I smiled at each other awkwardly. I thought of a picture

Danielle had once drawn of a mermaid drying her curls with a fish hair dryer. The mermaid had a wardrobe of shell brassieres and a chest of drawers full of boyfriends. One drawer was open, lined with men. A second drawer, closed, was marked simply *Chad, Tim, John,* and *Andy.* Perhaps I could be a mermaid by making believe. Before I'd met Thomas I was the least experienced person in the world. Through our role-playing I'd since spent time inside the skin of every slithery girl I'd ever met. I smiled again at Malcolm. "Say something," a voice told me, "make conversation."

"I guess you never really know anyone."

"No," Malcolm answered.

"You stand throwing wishes at another person!" My voice caught. "Wishes like old coins piling up at their feet, and they don't even bother picking them up!" I shook my head, to lose the image of Thomas's face. "Tell me what you do to kill time?"

He exhaled slowly. "I write a lot of poetry."

I crossed my legs. "What do you write poetry about?"

"The girls I fall in love with." He glanced at me. "No. I'm being flippant. I've just finished a suite about the girls found in Belanglo."

"Oh. Doomed girls."

"Yes. Doomed girls."

In May last year, a road worker had been arrested outside Sydney for serially killing backpackers. He had taken pictures of himself, which the newpapers later printed, dressed as a sheriff with his huge handlebar mustache, holding a gun the size of a water pipe. People, disgusted, went on and on, once again, about how Australia had forever lost its innocence. The man would pick up backpackers from near a Sydney youth hostel, and drive them to the middle of the Belanglo State Forest. Setting his victims free, he'd then hunt them down, severing their spinal cords so they'd be incapacitated while he was torturing them—one backpacker's head he used as a target practice; he shot at it from different directions within the forest. The police finally pinned the crimes on him by raiding his house, and finding he had the sleeping bags of two English girls, the cooking equipment of a German girl; his lover was wearing all the girls' clothes.

"Have *you* ever thought of going overseas, backpacking?" I asked.

"No," Malcolm said. "I have a sense, I guess it's superstitious, but—" He paused. "I feel that I will never leave Tasmania."

"Oh, I'm sure you will."

"I hate it, but I'm tied to it." He laughed bitterly. "I can't leave."

"What if you saved up very seriously?"

"Perhaps." He started lighting matches and dropping them into an ashtray.

"Not that I think backpacking is all it's cracked up to be." I was trying to brighten the mood. "My cousin went away last year, and came home completely depressed. Wherever she went she only met other Australians. All they talked about was their sore feet, and the girls kept bitching about her for packing a hair dryer." Malcolm continued lighting matches. It was a form of punctuation: he'd listen in a slightly morose way, then strike for the sulphuric pause. I shuddered. "It sounded awful. Washing out your underwear, hanging it up in little rooms . . ." I was about to die, yet I was counseling him on seeing the world.

Around us the men were growing restless, calling out for the barmaid. Eventually she reappeared, holding a recipe book, and filled each glass swiftly like a nurse on a casualty ward. Some spirits in dusty bottles had turned up, condensed like old cough syrup. In a plastic jug, she paddled the ingredients with a wooden spoon. All the drunks made wisecracks about wanting to be spanked. The barmaid poured her concoction into a wineglass, then added a tiny pink umbrella. "Sorry, love. No olives today."

I took a sip. I'd seen people with martinis in the films, and had not remembered the drink being green. "It's delicious!" I pronounced giddily. Malcolm smiled, and I closed my eyes. All around was a dull rumble. It sounded so familiar. There was a clinking of glasses; coins in someone's palm; the low, throaty hum of old smokers talking. "The noise sounds very close."

"It is very close," Malcolm replied.

I dissolved into giggles. Each action had become its cartoon. I leaned forward too close to hear him. I slammed down my glass as if trying to convince it to follow instructions. Malcolm lit another match and I grabbed him by the shirt. "Kiss me!" He burned himself. Shaking his hand he winced, then slowly a smile spread. With his good hand he took my wrist and kissed it gently on the inside. Behind us I heard laughter. "Kiss my mouth!"

"Not here." He was staring at the horse race as if suddenly worried. He watched intently, but his responses did not accord with the others' whoops and curses. A crazy old drunk, with long hair and a long beard, followed the action, his expressions those of someone in the pulpit. One finger was raised to the screen, like God pointing to Adam. His clothes were falling off him. Rubber bands held his trousers tight at his ankles. The man turned to me, winking, and mimed sitting on top of a horse in the rude way. Malcolm caught this routine. "That guy must have worked down a mine," he said softly, nodding to the anklets. "They'd do that to stop the rats running up their legs."

I leaned close to him, sipping the martini, twirling the little pink umbrella. "Drinking this makes me feel all funny. When I finish it, will you take me home with you?"

He looked over his shoulder. "Could we go to your place?"

"It's not safe."

He paused. "Well, it's just I live with my folks . . ."

"Do you have a car?"

"Yeah." He sounded impressed. "Yeah, I could take you for a drive."

I put my hand inside his pocket. "If you take me for a drive, I'll do whatever you want. I'll be your private slut."

He spluttered beer all over the bar. "That's what you tell half the blokes in town."

I giggled. He wiped the spill with a napkin and then looked around the room. I saw him catching the eyes of the other men. I stopped laughing. Malcolm had the softest Adam's apple and the dustiest clothes. I didn't know if he was too young for me or too old. And the more I thought of it, the more I imagined him, with his sweet face, modeling for the *dark angel* series one finds in true-crime novels: the murderer on the day of his first communion, standing with short pants lighting a candle; a dark-eyed misfit, in his wide-collared tuxedo, about to be rejected by the prom queen and all her ladies-in-waiting. My hand was stroking his thigh. "Tell me a line from one of your poems," I whispered. I could picture him in his bedroom with a photograph of the prettiest of the slain backpackers; the one he really wrote poetry for. "Tell me a line and I'll pretend to be your doomed girl." He was silent. "In the backseat I'll black out," I said. "Or, you can tie me up. We could fuck in the boot of your car."

Malcolm removed my hand. He scowled, but his forehead barely creased. "Listen, I think you're a nice girl." His throat trembled. "I saw you with the children in your class, and I know you're a nice girl."

Humming, I twirled the pink umbrella.

"Look, it's not a problem. It doesn't bother me you're"—he swallowed—"*into* that kind of stuff. It's just not my thing." Behind us a man walked out of the restroom. Malcolm turned to greet him enthusiastically, then he looked back into his beer, sheepish. "Your phone number is in there on the wall."

I paused a moment too long. "Does it say I'm a nice girl?"

"I'm serious," he whispered. "It describes you. It gives"— he cleared his throat—"your coloring."

"Only my coloring?" I pouted.

"Actually, I'm surprised no one's called late at night to tell you what it does say!"

I stood up, but felt myself sinking. I saw the sharks' jaws mounted on the wall and felt myself falling. "Are you all right?" His voice sounded far away. Outside the mackerel sky revealed its slipperiness. But inside, blue washed over the tables, the chairs. Surrounded by pieces of boats, long wrecked, were we actually underwater? I took a slow heavy step and heard laughter. All the rumbling sounds were close up. Everything faint now rang in my ears. A school of tiny, bright fish swam past me, following each other in a straight line; they changed direction suddenly, as if negotiating a sharp corner. But of course—I was in a box of blue water. People were hovering on the other side of the pane. I could feel the gaze of bloated strangers. It was no big deal: I was drowning while everybody watched.

"And what should I laugh at?"

The old kookaburra saw Miss Byrne stumbling around Lucien's house. Kingsley's beak no longer shone jet, and the royal blue of his plumage was fading; still, he knew trouble when he saw it. "That lad's teacher is behaving very badly," Kingsley spat. "If Lucien's parents separate, the child could suffer years of reunion fantasies—believing all the time if he had behaved a little better, if he hadn't asked so many questions or fussed over his chores, his mummy and daddy might've stayed together! If Mr. and Mrs. Marne divorce," the kookaburra screamed, "their son will proba-

bly flunk out of school, having learned too early he has no control over the world around him!"

Kingsley turned sharply. He heard it. The rutting.

In the branch above, two pygmy possums, their infinitesimal parts barely swollen, made ridiculous grunts. One branch higher were brushtail possums. These simpering creatures all had cat faces, but were centaurs below the waist. Launching themselves from drey to drey, the filthy acrobats spread their limbs, rubbing scalding secretions under the chin, the chest, around the anus to mark their territory. The kookaburra tried to concentrate on the prowling schoolteacher, but it was nigh impossible. The honey possums, with their extensile tongues, were lashing the nectar from every sweet blossom. Sexually dimorphic, their females were bigger than the menfolk, taking what they wanted from these gigolos with unsated itching lust! Echoing all around were the screeches of worlds ending. And everyone expected him to laugh it off: "Merry, merry king of the bush is he!" But his flunkies and lackeys, all of them were fornicating. Oh, this tree, his palace, was a bestiary! Each branch strained and groaned— the din would deafen him!

Kingsley wrapped his wings around his head. He felt his feathers wet with tears before he even realized he was crying. The bushland gang on the ground below: all of them were like displaced nobility. The weeping kookaburra turned, and on a nearby leaf saw a worm sitting by himself. "Come, let's away to prison," the old bird whispered. "When thou dost ask my blessing, I'll kneel down and ask of thee forgiveness." His stomach slack-

ened. "So we'll live, and pray, and sing, and tell old tales, and laugh," he told the worm, ". . . and take upon's the mystery of things as if we were God's spies." Kingsley thought of Terence Tiger with his old-world dignity. The thylacine kept his coat superbly clean despite his poverty, but did he not realize that in the future there wouldn't be detection as he'd known it? Sleuthing would be left to the scientists, rushing to the crime scene to get everyone's DNA. "Oh," the bird whispered, "and we'll wear out, in a walled prison, packs and sects of great ones that ebb and flow by the moon . . ."

Through his tears, Kingsley realized the boy's schoolteacher carried a knife. It glinted in the moonlight as she walked through the Marnes' garden. "Lucien," the kookaburra cried, "Hide! Hide!" Above, clouds were backlit by a moon-face dumb with pleasure. Cloud-lovers kissed; cloud-lovers fought; then there was the very sharpest of cloud-weapons. Kingsley Kookaburra groaned: "Why should I laugh?" he asked the worm. "And what should I laugh at? Men and their pomposity? Should I laugh at men in their wretchedness? At their limitless capacity to ignore their own callow stupidity? I am an old king! I am an old king!" He raised his feathers till they fanned behind, a mangy ceremonial cape. "If I should laugh it will be because nothing," he cried, "nothing at all is even remotely amusing!"

It was difficult judging the distance of my feet from the ground and each step was heavier than I expected. The Marnes' house, white and modern, was immaculate but the garden overgrown. A dry branch grabbed at my ankle. I cried out, but Thomas's music was playing. It hid any sounds of drowning. I'd asked the children once what it would be like to live underwater. *What do you think you would eat? What would you wear?* At first their impressions were fairly standard: *We'd eat fish. We'd wear our bathing suits.* But before long, warmed up, all of them were straining their arms, hands in the air, desperate to give their impressions. The teacher would be a tortoise—a "taught-us." They would sunbathe on the waterspouts of whales. Survival only required buying gills from the kiosk, and once you'd dived down you'd see that *people who live underwater walk as if they are flying.* Mermen in seaweed suits hailed whale taxis. Mothers carried shopping bags made of woven fishbones. Octopus chefs sliced, diced, boiled, broiled. And old men tended their coral beds. *Underwater bullets can't hurt anyone,* but, just in case, prisoners were locked in sharks' jaws.

Henry had looked up at me, batting his lashes. "Can I write anything?"

"Of course you can write anything."

"Can I write this?" he'd added, smirking.

I'd looked down at his page: *Underwater I saw the techer with no clothes on.* "Teacher has an *a* after the *e*," I'd told him.

Walking through the Marnes' scratching grass, I now wondered how much of this disrespect had been based on evidence. In many of the children's opening sentences they had disposed of the school's teachers using a trained pack of killer sharks. *When they bug me I click my fingers and a great white takes chunks off them;* but even the greatest revolutionaries can't escape their bourgeois hearts. Although the underwater teachers had presumably all been fatally mauled, these fourth-graders still diligently went to school, and sat at coral desks writing on rocks with sharks' teeth. At lunchtime they planned to eat seaweed doughnuts. In music they would play the recorder: *a fish with holes in it.* During sport, everyone could catch the ball, because it would come toward them so slowly, *unless someone went fishing and popped it.* Then, at the end of the day, they'd ride whale buses home, or be picked up in underwater Ferraris that only drove at a few kilometers an hour.

A wall steadied me: through the Marnes' thin curtains I could count each petal springing from a vase; every detail on a chair's leg was carefully replicated. Their furniture looked like a cast of refined shadow puppets waiting for an audience. I continued following their side fence. The house was built on a slope. The back room was elevated and glass doors opened out onto a wooden deck level with my shoulders. Through a wide gap of curtain I could see the walls were perfectly white. There was not one painting. It was as bland as a hotel room or one of the serviced apartments where businesspeople stay. In one corner sat a blond-wood kitchen table, a set of chairs. In another, a navy blue couch and matching armchair taken straight from a catalogue. This furniture wouldn't get up to dance when the Marnes went to bed. The table and chairs clearly didn't have souls.

Thomas walked into the room. He picked up a glass and took a sip. It was the simplest thing anyone could do: I watched transfixed. Each muscle in his face, each tiny twitch, seemed unadulterated and therefore mesmerizing. He raised the glass to his lips, then turned sharply as if being called. He straightened up, but didn't move away. I wondered what I was seeing. He was as he really was, although he looked exactly the same. Thomas put the glass down and walked through a doorway.

I followed slowly. Trees, planted too close to the walls, scratched at my bare arms. "You have split me open," I whispered to him. The music he'd chosen was low and gentle. I clung to the dark wall and stifled a moan: close by, through a slit of curtain, Veronica was in their kitchen. She was taking white plates out of the dishwasher. She'd bend over to pull out a plate and would then reach up putting it inside a cupboard. She wore leggings and an oversized shirt. Her hair was pulled back into a loose bun. She was scowling. Thomas must have been standing there with her, for now she was saying something. She repeated the sequence, but he didn't move to help. She scowled again, as if listening, and picked up another plate. Then turning, the plate in her hand, she interrupted him.

Each different ending to *Murder at Black Swan Point*, I'd

imagined in the pub, was a Rorschach of Thomas's, Veronica's, and my separate desires. Veronica, her face furious and tired, was wishing now for her ending of choice. She had captured Black Swan Point's crime the way the camera can steal a soul, enlarging or shrinking any detail to suit her purposes. Investigating the Suicide Cliffs, her long hair billowing in the breeze, she'd meant to conjure the desperation a once-gentle woman would feel after committing a brutal murder. Veronica walked around, strangely cheerful. When she noticed an appropriate cliff she gave herself the thumbs-up. In her secret heart she imagined her antiheroine slaying the nubile rival with relish, then disappearing: Margot would fly to a safe sunny place for a new life, Medea rescued by the sun god, and she would never again feel cold, and everyone would love her.

Veronica took another plate from the dishwasher. Then another. Then another. Voyeurism turns on the slow burn of waiting for something to happen; perhaps all perversity comes gift-wrapped, so to speak, in the banal. I stood by a large lavender bush, watching her, as I inhaled lungfuls of cool night air. I can smell your flowers, I thought. In a secret chamber of my heart I wished Veronica had written an extra chapter. I preferred thinking that after the young girl was knifed to death, the wife came home, hoping to inherit her old life, and the grief-stricken husband put his hands around her throat and, as I've suggested, avenged the girl's death. While his wife was unconscious, he threw her from a cliff, so she could drown the way Ellie had drowned, when the knife blow to her chest filled her lung cavity with blood.

Veronica's face was angry. She threw her hands in the air,

shaking her head again, and again. Then she started on the cutlery. She shelved the teaspoons first, then the tablespoons. Being boring is the exhibitionist's alibi, but the Marnes were half-expecting me. There was an inevitability to this visit and the music had been selected to reel me in. It seemed to be saying, "Come closer and you'll know too." I ignored each note's little plea. I was visiting because it seemed only fair, given our entanglement, that they should learn first of my intention to leave Endport Primary School. There were endless ways the community could have found out about the affair. According to Malcolm, the pub's toilet wall intimated I was sleeping with half the fathers in Endport. In theory it could've been any disgruntled citizen who had been harassing me. Although this did not mean I suddenly trusted the Marnes; in fact far from it. Now that I would no longer be around to serve as a target, I worried for their son.

Turning from the window, I shook my head. There was no area for Lucien to play, let alone a swing or a trampoline. This house was no place to raise a young boy. It was severe and cold and symptomatic of the Marnes' parenting. Lucien gave new definition to the term "only child." His sophistication was the way he survived living with two adults, but uncensored, his desires were just as juvenile as anyone else's. When I'd asked him to describe life underwater he'd been leaning low, his head almost on the page. This was his secret business. This was his own true-crime story.

The polar icecaps melted and all the boats sank, and all the oxygen masks sank. Underwater, 4B went on a ride called Dead People. Mummies, ghosts, and skeletons off an ancient shipwreck came alive. A ghost gave Danielle face powder and lipstick made of toxic waste—DDT—so her face fell off in bloody, revolting chunks. Then one of the boys, Darren, wet his pants, and a mummy took a swordfish and cut Darren into tiny pieces for human sushi! OH NO! Alastair was crying like a girl, so a Hammerhead bonged him on the head, and ate him in one bite. (Inside the shark, Alastair found a bicycle and a horse; and also some other kids. Soon Anaminka was swallowed and they all had a play together.)

The water was full of blood, and eyeballs, and little bits of guts. Then the shark did a giant burp. (It was like a gale-force wind.) And Billy's body was smashed apart by sheer stinking-force! Eliza and Henry were just lying there like frozen pieces of coma. But luckily, all through this, I was holding onto the Hammerhead's fin. He took me to buy food and toys . . . And then, the next thing I knew I was a great big shark too. And it was like I was battery-controlled, destroying everything in sight. I was eating up my teacher and even my Mum and my Dad. (It was fun.) I just kept on gulping people and destroying houses until everything was gone, even seaweed. But then I heard a sound. It was Sir Henry Shark-Killer: the greatest shark killer in history!

Instead of guns we used stingrays. He threw one at me. I threw one back. He hit me, and then I hit him, and we both fell down. I thought I was dead, but I wasn't sure. I got up, so obviously I was not dead. Then all the water disappeared, we sprinted in the little bit of water to the human body shop . . .

A branch scratched at my face and again I felt seasick. I imagined taking my number to queue, along with Veronica and Thomas, at Lucien's human body shop. All the people who'd most recently fallen off cliffs would also be in the reception, jostling for their appointment; a screaming tangle of broken bodies. We'd all be blind because, according to Lucien, *sand wears down eyeballs.* Our skin so wrinkled, *tearing easily like wet paper.*

It was hardly unusual for a child to fantasize about his parents being dead. Orphanhood was *the* great daydream of independence. All the stars of children's literature roamed free. Tom Sawyer and Huck Finn set their own agendas. Pippi Longstocking, Christopher Robin, James of *Giant Peach* renown—there was a stray elderly aunt lurking in the background, granted, although you never saw any parents. I wondered what had really happened to them. At the school fair, when the children stuck their hands into the horror table's black boxes, whose severed ears and tongues did they imagine they were feeling? To the bystander all the little painted faces and pony rides might have seemed delightful, but a natural order had been inverted. Children's desires were prioritized for the day and a chaos had emerged. The epic chaos of children touching their parents' dead bodies.

Sir Henry Shark-Killer and I grabbed a heart each, and lungs, and a liver. Except there was just one problem: there were not enough heads at the human body shop. They had just sold the last one to him! He got a semiautomatic, and I just grabbed any gun not knowing what it was, and I pulled the trigger, and "Oh no!" It was a pop gun. He shot me and this time I was dead! I lay bleeding; "Et tu Brute!" I tried to call, but I had no mouth, just a hacked-off vocal cord!

Lucien had read out this epic tale, acting every line. The other kids had been in hysterics. It had been a huge hit, and all the while the boy had really been crying for help.

I watched Thomas: he was now standing in the large white room next to the stereo, holding his glass. Veronica was by the door, yelling at him. This seemed to be their standard pose and Lucien had been asking, "What about *me*? What about *me* in all this?" I had been so busy worrying for my own safety I had neglected his. Now I had half a mind to take him with me. When, in his strange story, he turned into a shark, killing his parents—and, yes, his teacher—could his logic have been that he would kill us before we killed him? His mother, with the crime photos pinned up around her study, acted as if the body in its most degraded, mutilated state were quite natural. After Lucien made the dream catcher to protect Veronica, I'd asked Thomas about her sleeping problem. "The only person who wakes screaming is Lucien." No wonder if he was worried the human body shop had just run out of heads.

I knocked at the Marnes' front door. A few moments later an outside light switched on and Thomas opened up. "Kate! Has something happened?" I shook my head, and he closed the door slightly. "Well . . ." His attempt at a smile failed, stuck in a wince, "can we go through it tomorrow?"

Behind him Veronica appeared. "Oh, Miss Byrne!" She shook her head. "Your timing is astonishing."

"Only under extremely rare circumstances do I visit parents."

"Is that so?"

"In this case, it would be unforgivable for me not to stop by."

Thomas frowned. "This might have to wait."

"Oh no!" Veronica pushed in front of him. "Please, Miss Byrne, do come in. We don't want your conscience burdened."

I cleared my throat and walked straight past her into their living room. There were no rugs, no books, no clutter. Rather than aesthetic, their minimalism seemed a clue that when they mobilized it would be swift. "Sit down," Veronica ordered, pointing to the navy couch. She stamped in the opposite direction, wearing old socks. Her walk was both jerky and feline, practiced and unconscious all at once. Turning back to Thomas, she asked, "Could you entertain our guest for a moment?" She opened the door to what I assumed was their bedroom, leaving us.

"Please," he said simply. "You have to go."

I sat down, putting a finger to my lips. "Wait. Wait. I came to say good-bye."

There was something in Thomas's expression that almost made me stand and run. I'd asked Eliza once what it would be like to fall in love. "I think it would be really disgusting," she'd guessed, "and after you'd kissed someone you'd vomit." Thomas looked so sad. Then he shook his head and in that moment his face grew stern. He had such a regular demeanor, such perfectly even features that he could make himself completely opaque, resolutely adult.

A door slammed and Veronica reentered the room wearing a black dress. It had fine straps and showed off her pale neck and shoulders. Free from socks, her toenails were bright red. Carrying cigarettes and an ashtray, she sat down next to me, making the couch rock. She sat slightly too close and lighting up, said, "You've been drinking, I gather. Another?"

"No." I straightened my skirt. "I can't stay long."

"Just indulge us." She looked over at her husband, who stood by the stereo turning off the music. "Darling, could you? A Scotch for me and also for Miss Byrne."

"No!" I raised my voice. "I'm sorry but I have something to say." I now had a mental picture of how their house was laid out. There was a small pair of sneakers sitting outside the room closest to the front door. "The main reason for my visit is to express concern for Lucien. I think he's showing signs of strain." Since there were so few furnishings everything echoed. "Is he asleep?"

"Did you want to say good night?" Veronica inhaled, then blew smoke toward me. "Listen, he'd love you to, but I think he'd just get overexcited. Are you sure you won't have a drink?" She flicked ash. "I wanted to make a toast; to thank you for all the help you've given our son."

I felt for my purse. "Obviously, Mrs. Marne, this is awkward for a variety of reasons, but I'm just going to jump in and say my piece." I glared at her. "Lucien's drawings are quite disturbing. He seems to feel he's in danger." The purse was nestled between the couch's arm and my thigh. "It's not unusual for children to think their parents, in the form of monsters, are trying to murder them." Veronica smirked and I opened the clasp, putting my hand inside. "I think you have possibly subjected your son to information inappropriate for a child. I think it is indecent of you to have left murder photographs around your house."

She laughed.

"If you had been responsible, Mrs. Marne, you would not have allowed him access to this graphic material." She was laughing at me. "And I blame you too." I looked at Thomas: if I started to cry would it arouse his sympathy or libido? Veronica kept laughing, and Thomas said nothing. I put my hand around the knife's handle. "You probably fuck all your son's teachers! You probably fuck all his caregivers to get better service!"

"The policy," Veronica muttered, "hardly seems to be working."

"You don't understand! Your child has been yelling out to anyone who'll listen, 'What about me!' He feels like an orphan. He feels like you are both trying to cut his head off!"

"Enough!" Veronica moved to stand.

"No!" I took out my knife, holding it forward, and she whimpered. "He just wants to be a child! Don't you see that? A little kid; but you are both tormenting him!" I rushed toward Lucien's room. I almost expected him to have his bags packed—he would be better off as far as possible from here. Throwing open the door, I found the walls decorated with posters of the planets. A mural of rocket ships, hand painted, hung from the center of the ceiling. To the right, there was a red bunk bed and bookshelves full of bright spines. To the left more shelves and a table, upon which the boy's drawing equipment was carefully organized. "Lucien!" I couldn't see him. "Lucien!"

The door of the built-in wardrobe opened. He walked out trying to muster the dignity of, say, a judge walking from his private chambers to the courtroom. Dressed, however, in light blue pajamas and a maroon dressing gown he looked too young and, at the same time, too rakish. One expected the crack of doorway to reveal flappers dancing, a gramophone. Instead what flashed behind him were board games and socks. I covered the knife with my beaded purse. He pretended to be looking at "files," blank paper he was holding. "Oh, hello." Glancing up, he acted surprised. "Why are you here?"

"Darling, Miss Byrne just stopped by for a nightcap!" Veronica quickly told him. "She wanted to wish you a good night's sleep."

"Oh, thank you." He held his head high, acting along. "Would you like a seat?" He gestured to a small chair.

"Sweetie, Miss Byrne has to be going!"

"Oh, I can stay a little while." I sat down, my knees bunched in front. I sat with my back against the wall, between Lucien and his parents. "You've been drawing?"

"That's correct." His hands were shaking. "This is the space station I have been designing. And this is their light-speed shuttle." On his table was a jar full of coins and paper scraps—IOUs all written in different colors by Lucien himself, as if he had a variety of commissions. He saw me staring through the glass and said, "For fifty cents I can draw you anything you want. Anything."

"Miss Byrne, it's really past Lucien's bedtime." Thomas's voice was hard.

"Draw me a picture of life underwater."

Lucien cleared his throat. "I guess I'll need the fifty cents."

"Oh yes." I kept the knife covered, fumbling open the purse with my free hand.

"Well, this has been lovely!" Veronica started. "But it's time . . ."

I put a dollar on the table. "And draw me a picture of yourself."

"Underwater?"

"However."

In the textbook they'd claimed that after the child stopped drawing fruit trees, and rainbows, if he trusted you, he'd draw the real story. They had shown a picture by an eight-year-old girl of her father hanging their family dog in a tree. They'd shown a drawing done by a seven-year-old boy, in the midst of a divorce; his mother and father were pushing him off a cliff. I'd read that once, when pressed by a psychologist on the police payroll, the daughter of a terrorist kept drawing bombs, "gift boxes" that her daddy had been making, eventually securing her father's conviction.

Veronica was clucking. "It's very realistic."

"Yes," said Thomas, "yes, it's good."

I watched on, disheartened: Lucien was drawing a shark in cross-section; he was humming to himself as he included the vertebrae, the heart, the gills, and then the stomach. "Mum and Dad, I'll be quick so you guys should put in orders as well." He smiled, playing the part of the child almost too convincingly. His room set the stage. The edge of his bed was lined with soft toys; the sheets were patterned with superheroes; stickers covered every spare surface. Smiling, Lucien goaded his parents: "I guess you could write IOUs." He was taking charge as if there'd never been a problem—his mother and father had not been fighting and I visited every other day. Lucien noticed me looking around and, in the shark's gut, he added a red bunk bed and a wardrobe. He then drew broken furniture spilling from the shark's jaws. "It's vomiting tables and chairs."

"That's where tables and chairs come from," Veronica said.

I gripped the knife. "I thought you were doing a self-portrait."

"Oh, I am." Lucien added a boy, limbless, floating with the furniture.

I stared at the drawing. All this gore was his equivalent of the fruit trees et cetera. I could have waited all night for him to draw the real story, but Veronica and Thomas were whispering behind me. "Tell me about your picture, Lucien," I asked quickly. "Is this boy happy or sad?"

"Well, he's not too happy I'd say."

"Is he unhappy on the inside too?"

Lucien looked world-weary. "Probably he'd be bleeding a lot."

I paused. "What is good about him?" There was silence. "What is bad about him, Lucien? Has he ever felt too sad to play?" Veronica stood between her son and me. "Does he ever feel too sad to sleep?" I was screaming now. "Does he ever have nightmares?" Thomas had put his hand under my arm, and was yanking me to my feet. I raised the knife.

"Kate!" Thomas growled. "Put it down!"

I stared at the knife's blade; then at Thomas's face, distorted like the money shot. His face was huge and angry in the second before he forced me into a headlock. I was gasping, struggling. "Let me go!" I felt I was inhaling water. "Let me go." I needed to breathe, but he only held me tighter.

"Put the knife down!"

I dropped it. "Please don't kill me!"

"Oh, for Christ's sake!" Thomas released his grip. "*Shut up,* will you?" I half-skidded, half-lurched toward the bunk bed. Then he took me by the hair, pulling me out of his son's bedroom, through the room with no rug, to the front door. In seconds I was on the ground, tasting dirt. I looked up. Behind Thomas rose his white house. Each window was now illuminated; light rolled off the tip of every leaf. "Kate, not all things have to be so momentous!" Thomas yelled. Veronica stood watching from the doorway, her hand over her mouth. Thomas made a sound like a dog in great pain. Then, he stood up straight. His expression stunned me: in his secret heart he imagined Graeme Harvey knocking off this whining girl who'd started to make trouble for him with his family. Then, coming home, he'd seen his furious wife, and thought, Well, while I'm at it. He'd have gone to bed with blood on his hands, but woken up a single man. "Now go! Get away from here!" Thomas snarled at me. He turned and pushing Veronica inside he slammed the door behind them. I lay on the ground: I was the only one to see the small silhouette, standing watching from the window.

· MURDER AT BLACK SWAN POINT ·

The bushland gang were watching over him.

Lyrebirds danced and the wind through their feathers played a lullaby silvery sweet. The red-throated whistler, the gray-crowned babbler, a reed warbler, rock warbler, and golden-headed fantail perched on a branch outside Lucien's window, singing their friend to sleep. As the little boy's eyelids fluttered, as he floated on the edge of dreams, the bushland gang watched over him. Terence Tiger, a twinkle in his eye, held Kitty Koala's paw steady. "Wouldn't it be lovely," the old bear whispered, "if there were some recipe to avoid becoming an adult. If only Lucien drank a magic potion, he could crawl inside the pages of his favorite fairy tale to receive three wishes. To eat chocolate cake for every meal. To have a team of invisible animal friends with special powers."

"In his dreams he can, Kitty," the tiger said wisely. Then he turned to the window and murmured to the sleeping child, "Stay with us, Lucien. We will protect you." In all his years of detection, Terence had often found grown-ups to be the greatest mystery of all. He smiled. "Kitty, my dear, that trifle looks heavenly."

A magpie, in tails, offered lavish dishes of dessert and kept each goblet full of lemonade. There was Wally Wombat! There was Kingsley Kookaburra! Oh, there was Percy Possum, charming all the youngest honey-possums with his rooftop adventures. . . . The lyrebirds ended their melody and curtsied with grace. But the entertainment was far from over. Nearby ran a little stream, and a band of musical frogs emerged from the water—one, two, three, four. The tallest stood on his hind legs, conducting. The next frog did a little drumroll. Another played a bright orange trumpet flower, his friend, the accordion. Oh, what a fine sound! The noisy friarbird held her tongue and the crimson chat fell silent. The moon made a smoky spotlight and every creature gasped: the black swans had arrived, in feathers and red heels, their bills painted a shocking scarlet.

"No more detective work tonight," Terence announced. "Only merrymaking!" He turned again to Lucien's window. "In the end, no one really knows what happened at Black Swan Point—only the god of wildebeest and butterflies. The unfortunate truth of true crime," he admitted, "is that, often, there is no ending." Now the tiger faced his friends and colleagues. Raising his goblet, he called for the show to begin.

Through the dark hush the swans cast their spells with voices smooth and rich. Swans mate for life and a dashing fellow joined each lady. "When all little creatures are tucked up in bed," cooed this gleaming chorus, "dozing the sleepy-sweet doze of the dead, the ax starts in snoring and grinding its fang. The dagger stoned on lullabies quits his harangue." The males' long necks wavered in the breeze. Then all the ladies kicked up their high heels, revealing a shock of soft white under-feathers. The beat became jaunty. "When you hear the noose yawning it's time for nigh-nigh! Why, the gun's in its holster, shooting dreams through the sky!" Oh, such a swan song had never before been heard!

Now all the animals joined in: feathers fluttered in every wild rainbow color. A line of wallabies joined tails, raising their paws. "Goodnight little convicts in lands near and far; spread out your hands to form a star! Wave twinkle-twinkle from side to side, you run from sweet slumber but cannot hide!" A spangled drongo and a shining starling flew through the night sky. "Sleep tight, stately tiger. Bon nuit, blind old bear. Mad kookaburra, return to your lair. Lie down little possums, and dream if you dare. Gute Nacht to adulteresses everywhere!"

It was Monday lunchtime before I drove past Port
Arthur along the road leading to Point Puer. To reach the
cliffs I parked before the point, then walked down a fern-
lined track. I inhaled deeply, and on each out-breath braced
myself. First thing that morning I had been invited into Lillian Hurnell's office: Lillian sat at her handsome cedar desk,
blushing. In front of me she placed a handwritten petition
calling for my dismissal. All the parents had signed, except
for the Marnes; but Lillian promptly provided another letter,
typewritten on stationery from Thomas's legal firm. "Lucien
will not be in school today nor tomorrow. The Marnes are
returning to Hobart." She hesitated knowingly. "I gather
they'll put their son back into his old school." Behind her
were sepia photographs of her thin-lipped ancestors looking
disappointed. "The Endport Primary community would
obviously like you to leave as soon as possible, but I've told
them I can't get an emergency teacher down here for at least
a week," Lillian complained. "If not two."

I assured her I would be gone by the end of the day. All I
needed was a few more hours with the children. My grandparents' house had been vacated. I'd drawn the curtains. I'd
turned off the power. And I'd decided, in another life, to

write a book-length explanation for Lucien: a child's book of
true crime. Apparently in Stalinist Russia, blacklisted writers
and artists had embedded secret messages in children's literature. Beautiful books were created, full of allegory, and the
adults would read them before bedtime and remain fast
asleep; disguised as the naive, subversive content was unrec-
ognizable. Children, hearing snoring, would gently take the
books from their parents' hands. They'd turn out the lights
and shut the doors, then tiptoe off to read the real story.

"If you wrote a book for children," I'd once asked Lucien,
"what would it be about?" His eyes had become bright. "I'd
do a story with a twist in the end."

I walked into my classroom as nervous as I had been for
my first class. Monday morning with all its new-leaf status:
clean clothes, shining shoes, the marks of the comb dragged
through wet hair. As was their ritual, the children sat in a circle on the floor. Usually first thing, we held Show and Tell.
Now I thought their chatter would be too much to bear. I
wasn't sure I'd be able to listen to them speak. Even children's
lies carry an uncanny clarity. Children understand intuitively
the interconnectedness of unlikely narrative strands. Their
stream of consciousness monologues meander right into
what everyone else is thinking: a closer and more painful
approximation of the truth. It should just be Show, experience had taught me. No Tell: otherwise the kids have too
much sovereignty. Go around the circle with button-lipped
children, get them to hold up their new money box, the scarf
they're knitting, the insects they've suffocated in a jam jar—
make up your own story.

"Guys, we might skip Show and Tell this morning . . ." I

waited for the kids to groan. "To have a debate!" My voice cracked. Only the faithful had made it to my class. The epithet still scratched on the door—I KNOW—I now claimed as my own. It was clear the children were aware of my dismissal: they were perfectly polite. They'd decided there was no longer a point in saving their civility for a rainy day. I was given respect, like a condemned man receives his favorite meal. At the end of the afternoon I'll be gone, I thought, and you will never see me again, but you'll hear stories. Most of which will involve my being on good terms with lying. Before I left I wanted to make a deal with them. I had asked them to think closely about their lives. In exchange they had to explain to me what had just happened. I needed to hear, one last time, all the things they thought. I needed to hear what they still believed in.

According to my watch there were two hours before lunch for a high-speed metaphysical experience. "If people told the truth all the time," I asked, "would that be a perfect world?"

> Henry: *It wouldn't be perfect, because just say you murdered someone, then you'd say, "Oh, I murdered someone today," and you'd just go straight to jail.*
> Billy: *But you'd normally only say that if someone asked. [Indignant] Your mum's not going to come up to you and say, "Oh, did you kill somebody today?"*
> Anaminka: *But she might say, "What did you do today?" and you'd have to tell the truth.*
> Billy: *You can't really make a perfect world, because there are robbers. And the perfect world for a robber would*

> *be to steal everything and to take all the money in the*
> *world. But everyone else would have different*
> *opinions . . . You couldn't create a perfect world that*
> *everybody likes.*
> Henry: *And another thing, we can't just make ourselves*
> *be perfect, because we don't have the genes of perfect*
> *people.*

The boys and girls sat on opposite sides of the room. I had the feeling that time had skipped too far ahead of us. These children who'd known each other since birth, who'd been in the same class since kindergarten, had suddenly developed a gender allergy. Eliza with her bowl-cut hair wore a ring, "so no one will think I'm a boy." Henry had had his curls shaved, "so no one thinks I'm a girl." Every Monday I noticed that the children had grown further over the weekend. "Stop!" I now felt like pleading. "Just wait another moment." Alastair, whose face was becoming longer, had suddenly given up sucking his thumb. Billy, having taken an interest in music, apparently listened to the Top 40 by himself in his mother's car. Danielle, with baby fat, wore cherry-flavored lipstick. But Anaminka, who was beginning to develop breasts, clung tighter to her favorite doll; she still believed absolutely in the tooth fairy.

> Anaminka: *If everyone told the truth there'd be no*
> *surprises. It would be pretty bad with everyone*
> *walking around saying the truth and nothing else.*
> Henry: *It's just fun sometimes to lie, to make jokes, just*
> *for tricks.*

The children discussed when and where it was appropriate to lie. They spoke of the qualities of lies. They spoke of the comforts of lying. This should have been a balm, and yet I sat back, pained slightly by their newfound maturity. An extraordinary calm seemed to have settled—with Lucien gone, the unwaged war was over. I stared around the classroom wondering why I'd returned. They were trying to console me, but what could they have possibly said to make things better? "You did the right thing." "You are no better and no worse than any of us." "We'll still be your friends."

The self-portrait wing now made me wince. The bookshelves lining the walls felt like padding in a cell. As soon as one started talking honestly to children, it became clear their literature was the true opiate of the masses. See the sun, blue-eyed and smiling; step inside a music box to hear the old melody of goo-goo, gaa-gaa. I had seen the scribble kids added to their fairy tales; I'd noted where they tore the pages. Who wanted to hear about hungry caterpillars when they were worrying whether God existed? The conversation rolled on and I looked out the window. "This book I'll write," I promised Lucien, "it will be as honest as the bushranger's diary of dreams. It will be the good-bye-to-childhood book; a book with pictures that is only meant for you."

The play equipment, without its cover of wriggling bodies, seemed severe. I studied a climbing frame made from giant tires, staring until finally I noticed something terrible. Like some macabre collage, this structure had been positioned next to a huge red fire hose. This fashion for children to climb all over enormous tires, to wrap themselves in the tires so they hung limp from the knees as if burning—was I the only one who found it in slightly poor taste? Children should secede. Their teachers were trying to induct them into an airbrushed prison. A world where people with walled imaginations lived walled lives. Children should take their packed lunches and run far away. The idea that they needed to be protected from the truth was surely a way for adults to protect themselves. The unseemly things which children said when left alone, when the brakes were taken off their aggression, were perfectly natural. They were the shadow-feelings of adults.

Shouting broke out: our rapprochement had proved too much for the less sophisticated kids; Darren had called Alastair a girl, and he had started to cry. We discussed that it was not a statement of truth that Alastair was a girl. And Darren apologized with mock sincerity. Everyone then sat waiting, expecting me to speak. It seemed I should leave them with something. I took a deep breath, and tried to advise that the most important thing was to always remain true to oneself.

Billy: *But sometimes when people tell a joke you have to lie because if everyone's laughing and you have no idea what they're laughing about, you just have to laugh with them.*

Miss Byrne: *If everyone else threw rocks, would you throw a rock as well?*

Henry: *That's not lying. Throwing a rock isn't lying.*

Miss Byrne: *But if you laughed, were you being true to yourself?*

Billy: *You feel a bit embarrassed though if you've no idea what everyone's laughing about and you just sit there.*

Miss Byrne: *It sounds like you think there are white lies,*
as well as black lies. And maybe gray lies.
Eliza: *And pink lies.*
Billy: *And yellow lies.*

And they all yelled out the colors of their favorite mis-
truths. I sat still and let this rainbow arch over me. I admired
their slapdash sense of morality. Their mix of amorality and
integrity. Their innocence and sophistication—in essence, the
childness and adultness of them. Their advocacy of balance
seemed quite sensible: you couldn't have too much lying, and
you couldn't have too much truth. Not too much good, nor too
much evil. I thought of the last few days. You couldn't have too
much dream; and no one should have too much reality.

The bell rang but the children were slow to join the others in the playground. Perhaps they sensed that when
they returned I'd be gone. Clutching her lunchbox, Eliza
approached my desk. She stared down and said sadly, "You
can't make a perfect world, I don't think."

"You might be right, Eliza." Leaning over to shake her
hand, I tried to smile. Each child then came forward and, one
by one, they put their hands in mine. I pretended we were
delegates at a special conference, one that had tried to
explore the nature of truth. "Plato believed that in an ideal
society we would be ruled by philosophers." There was a
tremble in my throat. "If I could make a perfect world," I
promised, "you guys would get the top jobs."

All of them were pleased by this possibility; they were
already doling out its privileges as they each passed through
the vandalized "door of knowledge." In seconds they would

be screaming down the slide. They'd be bellowing from the trees, playing a game involving twigs with made-up rules. How many of them could legitimately claim I KNOW with any glory, I didn't want to speculate. Some had learned things in my class; others had just felt the labor pains. To them I whispered: "May you never know." I thought of Lucien. Thomas and Veronica might have been open with each other all along, but their son had discovered I had a sex apprentice-ship with his father through his classmates. How convenient to have imagined they would not find out. *Children find out!* Children should have their own intelligence agency. They're the greatest eavesdroppers, the greatest spies: they watch and sense what's really going on, reading every nuance.

Removing my desk drawers I dumped any evidence into the bin. I swiftly wiped from the blackboard every trace of my hand. Then I stood in the doorway looking back at the classroom. Last Friday, during lunch, Lucien must have taken a key so as to scratch with fear, with fury, with glee his message to me, as I lay on a four-poster bed, pretending to be someone else. I had realized that I was not the girl in the book. Veronica and Thomas's relationship may have mirrored the ill-fated Harveys, but I was not Eleanor Siddell. She could have been played by the last girl Thomas had humili-ated his wife with, or perhaps the girl before that, or the girl to come. Doomed girls, all over the world, kiss good-bye the ones they love to go and practice brinkmanship. What these princesses afraid-of-nothing do not immediately realize is that they are leaving home to learn fear. Eleanor Siddell left her father's house, "but how far have I come," she mused, "living in his other house?" No wonder she wanted to get a little bit killed. She wanted to kill off the part of herself that was weakest: *Close my eyes, so I won't see this rosebud wallpaper I picked when I was seven. Kiss me and take away the china ornaments. Instill oblivion in every fornication; make me like a missing person, in your secret way, only promise to bring it all back after so many minutes.*

Lying all around Point Puer were bricks. Every few steps I came across another orange-yellow brick made by the boys. This site would have been the perfect place for a stoning, were it not so serene. Agapanthus sprung up, purple and white; wildflowers grew all around the rubble; a pond was covered with water lilies, each petal still more exquisite.

I felt it shouldn't be so beautiful, but it was. I felt I should imagine the boys stepping from the ship's hulk, taking their first drunken steps, but my mind rebelled. No one now really knew how the children's prison would have looked. On the western side of Point Puer, over the water, lay Port Arthur and, along farther, Dead Island, with its eucalyptus and gravestones. The point itself had a blink-and-you'll-miss-it quality. The remnants of a granite wall rose to support nothing. A stone basement was full of leaves and dank rainwater. The bay in which the convict children had washed was pure primary blue, but beside it piles of their bricks were cordoned off with wire and the yellow tape of a crime scene.

This was where bad children ended up. I walked toward Point Puer's eastern side, along the track leading to the Suicide Cliffs. As a child, I'd heard about the convict boys linking hands and throwing themselves to the sharks. Clasping a branch, I now took a step forward. Maybe the first stories we are told are the ones we find our way back to. "I often think of the old nursery rhymes," my grandmother told me before she died. *"Humpty Dumpty sat on a wall. Humpty Dumpty had a great fall*—all the men who rise so high fall down."

Cliffs unrolled in every direction. From a distance they claimed the same easy curves as the clouds above. Close up, they were stark vertical walls of granite; ramparts the waves had battered flat. Shelves of rock, like diving boards or planks, jutted from the cliff face. I stepped forward again. *"Hey diddle diddle, the cat and the fiddle.* Well, they've got cats now that can play a little violin. *The little dog laughed to see such fun, and the dish ran away with the spoon.* They can train dogs to laugh, you know. And I've seen the dish move away, just slightly, then the spoon stirring it."

At the very edge of the cliff, trees grew horizontally; the stone was pockmarked. Staring across the water, I turned back half expecting to catch a boy's shadow disappearing behind a tree. There was creaking in all the high branches, but the rock-a-bye babies were long gone. This book for Lucien: a bird would have to sing it to him. He'd have to walk outside one day and hear rain drumming or see the light slanted just so. In Russia when the adults had finally awoken, the story-tellers and illustrators had been punished, horribly. A famous artist was sent to Siberia, where she developed gangrene and lost both her legs. A writer, to avoid being captured, hanged herself in her apartment. Between each line in these books there must be another story, which has to be imagined, written in blood. Always true, this blood story will haunt you and keep you awake, and the grown-ups should never know of it.

Waves now rose like walls of glass, then shattered, leaving smashed shells—or the ground-up bones of suicides—by my feet. Wind stung at my face and I stood feeling faint. This was the windiest place in the whole world. Wind blew straight from Antarctica and still the horizon's line looked flat. From miles away all the waves rocked in with their ancient come-on, that old tease: *I-might-not-break.* If the sea is a crib endlessly rocking, don't tell me the bough won't rot, baby won't fall. How can you look down without some awareness of the end's proximity, and not be slightly seduced? Close your eyes: listen to the sea. You're so near to it—the cradle and the grave—even if you never want to die.

ACKNOWLEDGMENTS

The author gratefully acknowledges Doug Dibbern, Alex Halberstadt, John Wray, Juliet O'Conor of the State Library of Victoria, Nigel Hargraves of the University of Tasmania's Centre for Historical Research, and the very inspiring teacher and brilliant fourth-grade students who shared their philosophical insights.